THE SLEEPER

'We have a guy well placed in the Kremlin, Mr President. He supplies us with first-rate information, but he could never get his hands on advanced information such as this. So, how well placed must a guy be to get this kind of information in advance? Where does London get it from? Our guy's so well hidden we thought London would never imagine we had one there. We used him to check London's information in case they were trying to hold out on us, but it seems they've got someone deeper – which means they must know who our guy is. They've been stringing us along.'

The President knew only too well what it meant. It meant that London had to have a man in the Presidium of the Supreme Soviet.

THE SLEEPER

Michael Hughes

Star

A STAR BOOK

published by
the Paperback Division of
W. H. ALLEN & Co. Ltd

A Star Book
Published in 1981
by the Paperback Division of
W. H. Allen & Co. Ltd
A Howard and Wyndham Company
44 Hill Street, London W1X 8LB

First published in Great Britain as *The Sleeper Awakes* by
W. H. Allen & Co. Ltd., 1980

Printed in Great Britain by
Hunt Barnard Printing Ltd., Aylesbury, Bucks.

ISBN 0 352 30818 4

One

'I wonder does anyone use any of this?'

Gary Butler turned to his colleague Walter Merringer. He'd asked the question a thousand times.

'Hell, we'll never know.' Merringer always gave the same answer.

'I mean,' said Butler. 'Look at this crap.'

Merringer took the sheet of paper from Butler and read it.

'Christ, Walt,' Butler shook his head. 'Who the hell will want to know in twenty years time what the British Prime Minister wore during a visit to France?'

'I don't know, Gary.' Merringer handed back the paper. 'Someone must think it's important.'

Butler shrugged and shook his head.

There were seventy-two on duty at any one time, every one vetted and classified as security A-1; seventy-two men and women who fed the world's secrets into the giant Jones-Mollart computer, in the bowels of the CIA headquarters at Fort Langley in Virginia. In charge of the seventy-two were twelve supervisors, three superintendents and a single director, and to reach any of them from the street meant going through the most stringent security procedure in the world.

Reports came in continually, every minute of every day; they were coded by the analysts on duty, given a sequence coding for reference, and programmed for entry into the giant electronic brain. The reports came from every corner of the world, from spies and agents, from foreign embassies and diplomats. There was very little went on in the world that the CIA didn't know about.

1

'I'll do the RIP sheets now, Walt.' Butler said.

The comment was unnecessary. Butler always did the RIP sheets.

RIP stood for RECIPROCAL INFORMATION PACT, and meant simply that Washington and London shared information.

There were 126 RIP sheets, already titled with London's identification, now requiring Butler to transform the signals on the sheets into an instruction. The first RIP sheet was easy enough. He recognised the London reference. London always began ECB/4 HRT, then came the address, or sequence number. The first sheet was headed ECB/4 HRT96. To check that the previous sequence was unaltered Butler questioned the computer. He asynchronised the central processing unit and keyed in his own mnemonic. In a flash the visual display unit informed him that the machine was ready to receive.

His own mnemonic, 35 BIG JIBBY 19, gave him access to memory banks contained within a certain parameter. Without the mnemonic it was impossible for anyone to reach the banks.

The bank was split into sections, each requiring a mnemonic to reach its data stores – Butler could have as many as he liked – and when 14 GARDEN STATE 3 was entered the path to the data was clear. The asynchronisation was relieved and he keyed in LOAD.

The VDU immediately displayed the last RIP sheet to have been entered. He nodded when ECB/4 HRT95 flashed up. His mind a mass of terminology, Butler put the machine into asynchronisation once more. He could then feed his information in, and when the asynchronisation was again relieved, in an instant the information would be committed to memory within the data stores of the giant 'JM'.

ECB/4 HRT96 was a signal stating that the British Ambassador to Angola had established the presence of a further 6,000 Cuban troops in the country.

ECB/4 HRT97 to 100 also entered easily, then the sequence changed. At 100 the last letter went on to the next in alphabetical order, thus ECB/4 HRU began. HRU1 to 17 presented no problem, but where ECB/4 HRU18 should have been, there was a strange reading.

The sheet was entitled simply V/2157, and it had come from a computer.

> 'V/2157 ... RUSSIAN NATIONAL AND DISSIDENT ... ANATOLI PRUTESKAYA ... IS TO BE ARRESTED ... KGB ... SOON ... IN MOSCOW ... TRIAL TO FOLLOW WITHIN DAYS ... WILL BE FOUND GUILTY ... SENTENCED TO 25 YEARS HARSH REGIME. AFTER 3 MONTHS ... WILL BE OFFERED ... IN EXCHANGE ... FOR GERRY FAIRBROTHER ...'

'Hey, Walt,' Butler swung round on his swivel stool. 'Ever heard of Gerry Fairbrother?'

'Fairbrother?' Merringer looked up at the ceiling. 'Aint he the guy they put away for thirty years?'

Butler remembered. Fairbrother had been employed at a weapons research centre. Caught handing over secrets to the Russians. It had set back the Pentagon's target by at least ten years.

Butler swung back and stared at the sheet. He hadn't seen the coding before. The next sheet, he noticed, was in sequence. Somehow V/2157 had found its way among them. But from where?

He called over his supervisor.

Wayne Schumacker, a bulky, red-haired individual, approached.

'Trouble?'

'I don't know,' Butler handed Schumacker the sheet. 'This is a strange one.'

Schumacker read it and shook his head.

'Doesn't mean nothing to me.' He called over his shoulder for Jack Smith, his superintendent, to have a look.

Smith was baffled. The signal meant nothing, but the words excited him.

'Okay, Wayne. I'll have Ken have a look at it.'

Ken Lawrence, the director on duty was equally excited. He nodded to Smith who returned to his post and picked up a telephone.

Five floors above, Joe Mellini's telephone rang.

'Mellini!'

'Joe ... Ken Lawrence. We've come across something I think you ought to look at.'

'What is it?'

'You've got to come down for this one, Joe. It's something that can't go out of this room.'

'Okay,' Mellini sighed, then when he replaced the receiver he growled.

'Shit!' The last thing he wanted was a trip downstairs.

Mellini had served the CIA since the forties. Thirty-two years he'd slaved and studied to keep the world from turning red, but it was a losing struggle. Nicaragua, right on Washington's doorstep, had fallen. Next, he knew, would be Peru or Bolivia.

Mellini was fifty-four and looked fifteen years older. Lond periods in planes and on stake-outs had taken its toll. He'd gone to fat and his bright red face was lined with a crinklèd coarseness. The Agency's doctors were always warning him to take things easy or he'd keel over. His body had taken a lot of punishment over the years, they'd told him, and it could take only so much.

Mellini knew his days might be numbered. He was only five-five in his bare feet and weighed 198 lb; he tired easily, finding it difficult to breath at times. But, hell, it was his life. He couldn't do without the CIA.

He showed his pass to the armed guard who operated the elevator and stepped into the cabin.

'Which floor, Mr Mellini?'

'Three down.'

The guard nodded and closed the bomb-proof doors.

Mellini watched the indicator. In a second it flicked to 'GROUND', then three seconds went by while the elevator passed through 60 ft of reinforced carbonised concrete. The indicator flicked to 'ONE-RED', then to 'TWO', then 'THREE', and stopped. The bomb-proof doors opened and the freshness of the air-conditioning hit him.

'This way, Mr Mellini.' A sentry approached him.

This was the part he didn't like. He was 140 ft underground, the computer was barely a hundred yards away, but it would take him an hour to reach it. He'd helped devise the procedure for security. It was unique in its own way. But it was a cow to get through.

He knew it by heart but allowed the sentry on escort duty to put him through the paces.

'Your clothes, Mr Mellini.'

Mellini removed his clothing and, feeling embarrassed with his aged obesity, stood before the electronic monitors. He leaned forward and placed the palms of his hands against the scanning windows. The sentry pushed his ID card into a slot.

'Mellini, Joseph T,' the mechanical voice from the loudspeaker said. 'Affirmative!'

But that was only the beginning, Mellini sighed. There was a long way to go yet.

A hatch opened in the wall and two sets of red clothing flopped out. The escort sentry stripped alongside Mellini and together they put on the fresh clothing. It was simple enough dress. For men it consisted of underpants, vest, socks and plimsoles, and a body coverall, all of them red.

'Okay, Mr Mellini?'

They walked the twenty-five yards to the next control point, again which meant stripping, checking and changing, this time to blue clothing. Another twenty-five yards and into yellow clothing, and the final twenty-five yards in the standard green clothing. And at each control point going through electronically controlled steel gates.

It was the ultimate in security. No one, but no one, could infiltrate the computer room. The colour codes were changed every day and anyone foolish enough to attempt to bridge the gap between any two control points would be shot down – that is, if they got as far as the third level.

He'd helped set it up, but, Christ, he hated having to go through it all.

'Hi, Joe!' Ken Lawrence greeted him. 'Let's use my office.'

Lawrence's office was soundproofed and kept out the clatter of sounds and voices from the vast computer arena, but he could monitor any of the programmers during their shift.

'You recognise this coding, Joe?'

It did nothing for Mellini. 'Never seen it before.'

'What about the signal itself?'

'Yeah, it certainly poses a –'

A telephone interrupted him. It rang until Lawrence picked it up.

'Lawrence.'

'Chief,' It was Gary Butler. 'Something's come up. It's got to do with that strange RIP sheet.'

'C'mon.' Lawrence grabbed Mellini's arm.

Smith and Schumacker were already standing over Butler, staring at the VDU. 'INVALID ENTRY ... QUERY ... RIP SHEET ECB/4 HRU18 ... PROVISIONALLY V/2157 ... INVESTIGATE ... REFER RIP SHEET ECB/3 DM087 ... CHECK ... CHECK ... CHECK ...'

'What the hell's going on?' Mellini was mystified.

'God knows,' someone said.

Butler spoke up. 'I'm linked into a sub-routine for identification of duplications. I transmitted V/2157 as ECB/4 HRU18, and this came up.'

'Is the DMO sequence in the same area?' Mellini asked.

'No sir, but when I transmit I always go into duplex. It's in case a RIP sheet is duplicated in another section. I can take it out from here.'

Mellini understood. Butler could enter another section of the memory banks for reference without going through the complicated procedure of direct addressing. But it would only tell him where to check and not supply him with specific information.

'Okay,' said Mellini. 'Get into that section and find out what's gone wrong.'

Butler relieved the section, went through the procedure of entering the area containing ECB/3 DMO87, and brought the information both to the VDU and hard print-out.

'RIP SHEET ECB/3 DMO87 ... PROVISIONALLY V/2127 ... ENTERED JANUARY 26 ... 1973 ... 7.15 am ... EASTERN STANDARD TIME ... PYTOR KRASNOV ... EMINENT RUSSIAN WRITER ... AND DISSIDENT ... WILL BE ARRESTED ... IN MOSCOW

BY KGB ... ON MARCH 24 1973 ... TRIAL WILL COMMENCE ... IMMEDIATELY AND LAST TWO ... REPEAT ... TWO WEEKS ... KRASNOV WILL BE SENTENCED ... TO 15 YEARS ... IN PRETORKIV HARSH REGIME ... ON JUNE 17 ... 1973 ... KRASNOV WILL BE OFFERED ... TO WASHINGTON ... IN EXCHANGE FOR ... ARMAND GERMAIN ...'

'You don't recognise anything, Joe?' Lawrence asked.

'Yeah, I recognise Krasnov and Germain. I remember the exchange, but I sure as hell don't remember any information like this.'

They were all stunned, but not so much as Joe Mellini; for he was chief of European Operations and had engineered Washington's side of the deal.

'Okay,' he said, 'I want a print-out of both these sheets. I also want a copy of every scrap of information we have on Germain, Krasnov, Pruteskaya and Fairbrother ... in my office in two hours.'

Back in his office Mellini was furious with himself. He had actually arranged the Krasnov-Germain swop and saw it through to its completion, and Christ, the information had been received before any talk of a swap took place!

Who was 'V'? he wondered.

He flicked his intercom and spoke into it.

'Get me Ray Rogal, a car and an escort.'

Ray Rogal came into Mellini's office shortly afterwards. He was the same weight as Mellini, but eleven inches taller. He was broad, boyish-looking, his fair hair cut short and combed with a parting; still only thirty-eight he was waiting to step into Mellini's shoes. Mellini was on the phone speaking to Washington.

'Chief?'

'We're going to Washington, Ray. I'll tell you about it in the car.'

Rogal studied the sheets and blew through his lips.

'Jeez, wasn't this one of yours?'

'The same.'
'You didn't know?'

'They took me for a patsy. Christ! We kept it under wraps until they were changed over – both sides – it was top secret. And the God-damned reds had planned it all along!'

'How did we manage to miss the RIP sheet?'

'I don't know.' Mellini gestured hopelessly. 'But we did ... Christ, did we!'

The director of the CIA was already with the President, and Mellini's earlier telephone call ensured that both men would remain together until Mellini and Rogal arrived. Both senior men took it like a hard blow in the guts.

'You'd better fill me in on the details.' The President said.

'Mr President,' Mellini took the lead. 'You know about the RIP sheets from London ... Okay? ... The ECB simply means EUROPE, COLIN BALQUIDDER. He's the guy in London who sends us the sheets, works for a department of SIS. The other letters and numbers are just sequences ... Okay, we somehow missed this RIP sheet from seven years ago, and the Reds took us. Until now we thought we knew all the London codings ... but this here 'V' shows that we don't.'

'Can we be sure it is a coding that London uses?'

'I am, Mr President. Seven years ago we missed V/2127, and history has proved it to have been a hundred per cent correct. And these sheets come direct from London.'

'And you think this latest one will prove to be correct?'

'Yessir, I do, but there's more. Christ, it's deadly.'

'Go on ...'

'We have a guy well placed in the Kremlin, Mr President. He supplies us with first-rate information, but he could never get his hands on advanced information such as this. So, how well placed must a guy be to get this kind of information in advance? Where does London get it from?'

'Yes,' the President nodded. 'Follow you.'

'Y'see,' Mellini began to sweat, even in the air-conditioned office. 'Our guy's so well hidden we thought London would never imagine that we had one there. We used him to check London's information in case they were trying to hold out on us, but it seems they've someone deeper — which means they must know who our guy is. They've been stringing us along, making us believe we've been stringing them. Jesus, never in our wildest dreams could we ever have imagined they had a guy that deep in!'

The President knew only too well what it meant. It meant that London had to have a man in the Presidium of the Supreme Soviet.

Two

The President was staggered. Only a year ago he'd taken part in the SALT talks with Brezhnev. For the newreel cameras they'd done what was expected of them. But off-camera they'd spoken about other things; things which if made public would seriously damage America's image in Western Europe, and which now were evidently filed away somewhere in London. Whoever the guy was he would certainly have been at one of the meetings when they'd talked informally ... Jesus Christ!

The more the President thought about it, the more deadly it became. Moscow had spies in every country in the world, no matter how small, and all the information gathered was channelled back to the Kremlin and studied. Those sort of files Washington would have given a generation of fighting men to get hold of — which until now had seemed impossible — but London was in there picking up the points. London knew everything that Moscow knew.

It was a frightening prospect. As well as spying on the Kremlin, London was using the KGB to spy on her allies. Whatever information was gathered in the US and elsewhere ended up in London; which meant that Washington was an open house.

'It scares me,' the President admitted. 'London must have people inside our own CIA, and what with that and their guy in Moscow, there's nothing they don't know about.'

The CIA director was pale. All the implications were only too apparent. London held the world in its grasp and was quietly going about its business as if spying was something that only went on in other countries.

'I'm sending Ray over to England.' Mellini said. 'He'll find out who "V" is, then we'll flush out their guy inside.'

'Doesn't anyone have any idea who "V" might be?'

'He's an unknown, Mr President, part of Balquidder's section. We've been trying to penetrate Balquidder for years and had no success, but we're still working on it.'

'Is he inside?'

'No, sir. He's working on one of Balquidder's people. We don't think it's time to move him any closer.'

'I think you should move him in.'

'That could be a mistake,' said the CIA director. 'I'd like to wait until the right time, and I don't think the time is right yet.'

'What do you think?' the President asked Mellini.

'I'll take the chance, sir. The Chief's right, but in the circumstances I'd tackle it. We might never get another chance.'

'Then move him in.'

'I still say it could be a mistake.' The director warned.

'Get everyone available onto it. We've got to find out who they have in that God-damned Kremlin. What do you know so far?'

'Me and Ray worked out a few things coming here, sir. Most of it's pure guesswork, but some of it we're pretty certain about.'

'Like?'

'Well, sir, we reckon this guy sends out information only on infrequent occasions. He can't be too regular or the KGB would know there was a major leak. The first "V" sheet we got – the one we missed – shows the number 2127, and the second shows 2157. Now we reckon the sequence takes in only the last two numbers, which in seven years makes a total of thirty signals, an average of four-and-a-half per year. The "V"/21 we think is a coding of some sort. We're sure he doesn't send many signals, but we haven't a clue as to how much is included in his signals.'

Mellini was no fool. He knew espionage, and all his reckonings were right on the ball.

'We must find both of them, "V" and ... what shall we call him?'

'How about "Prairie Dog"?' Rogal ventured.

11

'Good enough,' the President nodded. 'What's your first move?'

'Ray will go over to England and visit Balquidder,' Mellini said. 'I plan to throw Balquidder off-balance. If he shows true to form we'll work on his people.'

'Be tactful.'

'We'll be careful, Mr President.'

'Will it be your first time in England, Ray?' The President spoke directly to Rogal.

'No, sir. I've been there several times learning the system. But I've spent most of my European duties in France and Germany.'

'Then let me give you some advice – advice I believe your colleagues will agree with. Have you met Balquidder?'

'No, sir.'

'Okay, under no circumstances underestimate the British. Your counterparts over there behave and conduct themselves like the impeccable English gentlemen you see in the movies, but don't – as some of our people have done in the past – think they're foppish. You'll find them charming – overbearingly charming at times – but don't be taken in. Behind the "old school ties" and "old-boy" networks they're as ruthless as anything the KGB can dish out. They'll fall over themselves to help you, and you'll believe that you're getting every assistance, but they'll be kicking you in the balls every minute.'

Mellini and the CIA director were nodding their agreement.

Rogal took his leave some time later and the three other men discussed him.

'It's an almighty task for his first operation in England,' the President said. 'I hope he's capable.'

'He is,' said Mellini. 'It was Ray who persuaded Termakov to come over, and it was he who persuaded the Czech colonel to open up. He's experienced, and we want him to take up London for a while.'

The President grimaced when Mellini mentioned the Czech colonel. It had been a feather in their caps when he'd come over, or so they'd thought. He'd given himself up to the British and London asked Washington if they wanted him. The CIA had jumped at the chance but it had taken some time for him to open up. Once opened, he'd flowed with information, but as the information came out it was discovered that he'd been a British agent for years. Nobody had noticed that London had handed him over too quickly ... The God-damned limeys always seemed to be everywhere.

He nodded. 'For Christ sake, watch whose toes you might tread on.'

Rogal flew into London's Heathrow Airport thirty-six hours later. He was alone and there was no car waiting to pick him up. It was the way he wanted it. Someone from the Russian embassy was always at the airport waiting to see who was being picked up by official cars.

He took the airport bus to the terminal in Cromwell Road and from there a taxi to a mediocre hotel in North London. It was evening and he relaxed in the hotel's bar for an hour, then watched some television before turning in. In the morning he contacted the embassy by telephone and asked for a meeting to be arranged with Balquidder first thing the next morning, then he took the rest of the day off to take in the sights of London.

October in London, he found, was none too bright, but nonetheless the group of American tourists he joined on the tour seemed to enjoy themselves. Rogal enjoyed the tour too. It was seldom he found the opportunity to explore a country as a tourist. London was steeped in history and the tour-guide gave a good account of it, but it was all to short. Several weeks would have been better. In the early evening he called the embassy again and an agency official informed him that a meeting was arranged for him at 9.15 am the next day.

The address given by the embassy was not in Whitehall as he expected but in an old building in Old Broad Street, close to Liverpool Street station, where an accommodation bureau had its main offices.

The street was filled with men and women going to work, heavy traffic blocked most of the smaller side-streets, and there was a queue outside the bureau.

It was vital that he did not have to wait, and to snarls and howls from the people already waiting he pushed gently past the head of the queue.

'Mr Rogal?' A young woman clerk asked from behind a desk.

'Good morning,' he said. 'Yes, Rogal.'

'This way, sir.'

He followed the young woman through a doorway, up a flight of stairs and into a room above the bureau. The young woman closed the door behind them and Rogal heard a distinct click as it locked electronically. The far wall quietly and suddenly slid away.

'This way, sir.'

He followed her along a narrow passageway for at least fifty yards, when she stopped outside a heavy door. The door swung open and on the other side was a waiting room.

'Please wait here for a few moments, sir,' the young woman said, and then went back the way she came, the door locking behind her.

The room was plush. No expense had been spared in furnishing it, but it had no windows and was obviously soundproofed. The previous day's edition of the *New York Times* was lying on a table. He took it up and sat down to read. It was twelve minutes past nine.

At exactly nine-fifteen another door opened and Balquidder entered. Rogal looked up and smiled. He knew full well that Balquidder had been studying him secretly for some minutes.

'Colin Balquidder?' He rose. 'I'm Ray Rogal ... Hi!'

'Good morning, Mr Rogal.' Balquidder beamed. 'How nice of you to come and visit us. Please come into my office.'

Rogal studied his counterpart quickly. Balquidder wasn't much older than himself. Perhaps two or three inches shorter, leaner, and like the President had said, he looked nothing like a spy.

Balquidder was immaculately dressed. His dark blue, three-piece pin-stripe suit looked as if it had been tailored just before breakfast. His brown and blue, angled-striped tie had the crest of a college sewn into it, and his white shirt dazzled with brightness. His black shoes might only have been for show they were so shiny.

Rogal noticed that the English didn't go in much for special

14

hairstyles. At Langley he could find a hundred different types of styling, but here in London the 'Gentlemen' all had the same. They all had short back and sides, a low parting and plenty of oil.

Apart from his clothes Balquidder didn't look much, he decided. He was too slim to be a fighter of any kind – all CIA agents were taught how to fight. His hands were like a young girl's, smooth and tender, and his two top teeth stuck out too much.

The office was as plush as the waiting room. It was furnished in the best leather and walnut, and Rogal bet that behind the panelled walls there was an assortment of goodies.

'Chilly morning, Mr Rogal, wouldn't you say?'

'A little,' agreed Rogal.

'Dashed parky ... However, you're just in time for tea. Would you like tea? Or perhaps you'd prefer coffee?'

'Tea will be fine, thank you.'

'Good show. On a morning like this it's best to start off with a hot cup of tea in the old tum. Please take a chair, Mr Rogal.'

Balquidder sank into an armchair that Rogal knew would have cost a thousand dollars apiece at home. Rogal accepted the invitation and faced his counterpart.

'And now,' Balquidder smiled, his hand folded on his knees. 'While we wait for tea perhaps you'll tell me the purpose of your visit?'

'Do you mind if we wait until the tea is brought first?' Rogal had to stall for a few minutes.

'By all means, old chap. No point in rushing things, what?'

'You have good cover here.' Rogal said, looking round. 'No one would guess ...'

'Yesss, it's had its uses. We'll be changing shortly though.'

'Closing, are you?'

'No, no. The owners wish to renovate the building.'

'Doesn't your department own the building?' Rogal asked with astonishment.

'Lord, no. We couldn't afford to buy property in an area like this. ... Ah, the tea.'

A middle-aged woman brought in a tray covered with silverware. It was 9.25.

'Toast?' Balquidder offered the rack to Rogal.

'Tea will be just fine, thank you, Mr. Balquidder.'

'Colin, please.'

'Okay, Colin,' Rogal smiled, and then chuckled. 'How you guys get any work done is a miracle. We have coffee breaks, yeah, but we don't sit down like this.'

Balquidder shook his head and tutted. 'Dreadful way to carry on. Gulping it down does one no good. And, if I might add, battles have been won and empires built over a cup of tea. A jolly good part of our heritage ... Jolly good.

It was 9.29.

'So, what brings you to London, Ray, old boy? Grosvenor Square arranged things yesterday, but didn't mention the purpose of your visit.'

'Well ...' Rogal kept his fingers crossed. He hoped Mellini would be prompt.

The telephone buzzed.

'Blast!' Balquidder rose.' Always happens, you know. Excuse me, old chap while I get rid of them. Shan't be a tick ...'

Rogal's eyes followed Balquidder. He watched the other's face as he walked to the telephone, but tried not to appear too inquisitive.

'Balquidder.'

Rogal watched him intently and tried to imagine the working on the other end of the line.

'Hi, Colin! ... Joe Mellini.'

'Good Lord. Good morning, Joe.' Balquidder was all smiles. 'I say, I've got one of your chaps with me now.'

'Yeah, he's over there to ask you about something. Well, I sorta got a bit impatient and thought I'd ask for myself.'

'Fire away, old chap. That's what we're here for.'

'Colin ...' Mellini paused. 'What do you know about the proposed deal between us and the Reds with Gerry Fairbrother and Anatoli Pruteskaya?'

'Prutesk ... I can't say I recognise the name, old chap. What was the other name you mentioned?'

Rogal cursed inwardly. Balquidder hadn't even blinked. He'd just gone on as if the conversation were normal. The rest of the discussion would be just a waste of time.

The conversation was short. Mellini accepted Balquidder's brief denial and mentioned that Rogal would do the explaining. He'd just got impatient, he said.

Balquidder came back to the armchair and sipped his tea, perfectly calm.

'Joe interrupted just as you were about to tell me ... He mentioned the name of some foreign chappie.'

Rogal took the 'V' sheet from his small attaché case and handed it over. It was the second trump card they could play. He watched Balquidder again.

'It concerns this ...'

Balquidder lay back in his chair and pushed out his bottom lip.

'Hmmm ... New one on me, old chap,' he read through it. 'Can't say I've heard of this Pruteskaya, but Fairbrother rings a bell.'

For an instant Rogal admired the Englishman. Not a flicker had passed across his face.

Balquidder handed back the sheet.

'Can't help you, old chap.'

'This came from London, Colin. It was among the latest batch of RIP sheets. The RIP sheets come from you.'

'Well, yes, old chap. I do send over the sheets, but I've never clapped eyes on this one before. Of course, I'd check it out if I were you. There might be something in it.'

He's good, thought Rogal ... God-damn, he's good!

He barged in. 'Cut the crap, Colin. We both know that this sheet got into the batch by mistake. Now, c'mon, this sort of thing worries us. Who's "V"?'

'Some more tea?' Balquidder was still the perfect host.

'Christ!' Snapped Rogal. 'Can't you guys think of nothing else but tea? What the hell are you letting us in for?'

'Ray, old chap,' Balquidder was soothing, but serious. 'I assure you that what you have there is completely unknown to me. I know no one called "V", and I haven't the faintest idea where it could have come from.'

'Come on! These sheets are untouched from the time they leave your office until they reach ours.'

'Precisely, old chap.'

17

'Eh?'

'I sign for the RIP sheets, and I personally inspect each one that leaves this department ...' He leaned across to Rogal to emphasise his point. 'And I still assure you that that wasn't there when I signed their despatch notice. I know nothing about it.'

Rogal stared at Balquidder. For a moment he began to doubt himself, but he remembered the President's warning.

'They were taken by diplomatic pouch to Grosvenor Square, old chap,' Balquidder went on. 'Perhaps one of your chaps made an addition?'

'The pouch was sealed, Colin. No one touched it until it reached its destination.'

'Maybe you have a secret benefactor?'

Rogal shook his head. 'No, Colin. You've boobed but you won't admit it. Now c'mon, don't frig us about. This is serious. If it's true about the deal, we've got to stop it before it evens gets off the ground. We could call the Reds' bluff right now.'

'I know nothing about it, old chap. Sorry.'

'Okay, Colin,' Rogal rose. He didn't mention the sheet from seven years earlier. 'I don't have to spell out for you what we know. So, if you won't help us, we'll help ourselves.'

'I'll give you every assistance, of course ...'

'Save it!' Rogal turned to the door, which opened suddenly to show the young lady waiting for him. 'You've damaged relations between us, Colin.'

Balquidder was a picture of innocence.

Three

Balquidder went into another office and from a window watched Rogal walk into the street. He waited until the American climbed into a taxi then went back to his main office. He pressed a button on his intercom and spoke roughly into it.

'Get me the entire staff in here immediately.'

When a staff meeting was called all doors on the floor were locked and all windows sealed. No chances were taken on anyone finding their way in.

'Last Thursday,' he said quietly. 'Someone made a cock-up. A "V" sheet somehow got into the latest batch of RIP sheets, and I've just had an angry visitor from Washington asking me about it ... Now!' His voice became angry. 'You are all going to go back to your offices and turn the clocks back to 8.45. You'll then go into the corridor, then go back to your offices as if you were starting in the morning, and before you open the doors you will make yourselves believe that it is last Thursday. You will simulate everything you did on that day, and discover how the cock-up was made. You will remember every tiny detail, however slight, and if you don't discover how the cock-up was made, you'll do another eight hours doing the same thing. And then again until we find out. Go!'

His staff, men and women alike, were shocked. They had all been hand-picked to serve on Balquidder's staff and they did their job with pride. Balquidder's tone did not upset them, but the fact that one of them, any one, had made a mistake, did.

They did not hurry. During their training they had often undergone simulated exercises, designed to trace the unlikelihood of a mistake. Their minds adjusted to the previous Thursday. All the clocks were turned back and as if acting out rehearsals for a play they donned their hats and coats and trooped into the corridor. A series of 'Good-mornings' were said and the real exercise began.

Balquidder locked himself in his office and opened a panel in a wall. Behind the panel was a lone telephone, one of a type of which only 102 existed in the whole country. It was old and still bore the dial of pre-STD days. When the country changed over to STD a section of the old system was taken out and formed into an independent, intruder-proof, security communication system. Very few people knew of its existence.

He dialled BAL 2291 and waited.

'Destination please?' A female voice said into his ear.

'The Vicar,' Balquidder replied.

Nothing else had to be said. Everyone along the system had a title and it was necessary to give only one's ultimate destination. It was not even necessary to give one's name and location.

It took a few minutes to raise the Vicar.

'Good morning,' the voice was soft and gentle. 'What can I do for you?' Balquidder gave a password and related his meeting with Rogal and the steps he had taken.

'Correct measures, Colin. It's serious. They know, and will pull out all stops to find our source. Investigate your end and I'll make one or two arrangements elsewhere.'

'Very good, sir.'

When Balquidder went back to his staff he found them quietly and methodically going through the events of the Thursday before. He admired them for an instant, as they talked about the television programmes they'd watched on the Wednesday evening. Mostly they could remember every detail, which was what they were trained to do, and when someone did make a mistake another would gently remind them of the fact. Balquidder took a seat and watched them. He didn't interrupt. He didn't have to. They knew what to do. But he watched just the same.

He watched Marjorie Atkinson first. Of the three women in the office Marjorie was the only one married. She was twenty-eight, married to her husband for five years. So far as reports

20

stated they were happily married. It was important that every member of the staff was happy in life otherwise their work could suffer; any lapse because of an emotional or domestic problem could prove catastrophic to the department. It was imperative that any member of the department who intended to marry went through the rigorous procedure of being vetted. They were vetted before they joined the department, but getting married meant their intended's background had to be investigated. It also meant that the couple had to account for their movements for two years beforehand. If the department were dissatisfied with what was revealed the candidate was asked to resign.

Marjorie and her husband had passed all the tests. They were both sound and emotionally suited. Neither complained at the measures expected of them during their courtship. They accepted that it was necessary if the security of the country was not to suffer.

Although she handled the signals when they first came in Balquidder doubted if she had made the mistake. Along with Norman Briscoe she decyphered incoming signals and analysed them, then passed them onto Charles Selfe and Johnny Trench for coding prior to entry into the computer. Marjorie and Briscoe did the job together, as was every task carried out in pairs. It was costly in terms of salaries, but when two people checked each other's work there was very little chance that anything could go wrong.

Briscoe was married too. He was forty-five and had been married fifteen years to a girl five years his junior, a teacher at an infant's school. He was steady and had initiative, like Marjorie he was ingrained with the necessity of mistakes not being made.

Selfe and Trench, thirty-seven and twenty-six respectively, were comparative newcomers to the department. They knew everything there was to know about computers. As Russian spies they could have become wealthy men. They had the access the Russians would have given a fortune for. Only they touched the keys on the console, in their heads were the mnemonics for entry to individual sections of the memory banks. One watched while the other entered the data, the other

21

then playing the feedback to check the entry. They never took chances.

They came well-recommended. Previously they'd been employed by the Government computing details of the last population census. Their expertise came to the notice of a security officer on the look-out for likely candidates, and during a quiet period they were invited to apply for positions in a department attached to the Foreign Office. Other departments had tried to get them into their ranks but the Vicar heard of them and whisked them away before anyone knew what was happening.

Sid Rainger and Eleanor Greenhill took the sheets from them. Sid and Eleanor retyped the information onto the sheets that eventually ended up in Washington, the first people to actually touch them. They did 'RIP', 'V' and 'TREFOR', one typing and the other checking, sorting them into small piles before passing them on.

Sid was twenty-seven, a product of Cambridge, who liked to spend his spare time building models of ships from matchsticks. He was due for replacement since letting slip that he had lost interest in what he did to earn his living. Balquidder had accepted the feeling and immediately a request went out for a suitable replacement. Someone in Sid's position was never encouraged to take more interest. He simply was no longer any good to the department and would be replaced soon. In that respect he could be a threat. He would not necessarily be aware of it but with his mind on other things he could make a tiny slip.

His partner, the youngest member of the staff at nineteen, appeared to revel in the job. Eleanor was a happy girl, always singing a popular tune, sometimes to the annoyance of the others. Balquidder remembered how he'd had to speak to her. Her choice in music was something to be desired. It wasn't music at all in his ears – Punk, she called it. It upset the others and she'd been told to stop. She changed to Country Music and there were no more complaints. Eleanor understood and appreciated the importance of the job, doing everything required of her for security, but she often teased the others and at times like that she could have made a mistake.

Len Earl and Derek Hannon had the sheets after Sid and Eleanor. They numbered the sheets, again one typing and the other checking. A list came from Selfe and Trench with the computer entries in numbered sequence. Len and Derek checked the information and sequence, and in the top right-hand corner typed on the relevant reference number.

Len Earl had been with Scotland Yard in the records office; a walking computer himself, he had a remarkable ability to remember details. He never, as yet, had made a mistake. At fifty he had thirty years' experience of records. Balquidder admired him as an individual worker and, side-stepping the rules when speed was important, he asked Earl for information off the top of his head. He checked afterwards to make sure and Earl was always right. He'd never have done the same thing with any of the others.

There was nothing he did not know about Hannon. Derek had been one of his junior officers when they served with the SAS, prior to being recruited by the Vicar. He'd have staked his life on Derek. They'd been in scrapes behind the Iron Curtain together and there had been times when they'd had to rely on each other. They'd come through safely, Balquidder leaving the service first and Derek two years later.

But both men handled the sheets. They handled them once the reference numbers were attached. The sheets were different colours and they weren't colour-blind. They talked while they worked. They did things automatically, sometimes not looking down to see what they were doing, relying on the other to make sure no mistakes were made. But what if the other missed something?

The last pair, the longest-serving, performed the task of checking again that sheets were in their right order and in their right piles. Shoulder to shoulder they took the different piles of sheets to the VDU and ticked off every item, then returned to their desks and prepared each pile for despatch. 'RIP' sheets were placed in a sealed envelope for Washington, 'TREFOR' were placed in separate sealed envelopes for another department in Whitehall, and 'V' sheets were handed back to Selfe and Trench to be processed through the shredder.

Patricia Birdsall had worked all her life in Intelligence. As a teenager at the time of the Korean War she'd been recruited by the Vicar's people of the time, years before Balquidder. Convent educated she'd never had a lot of contact with the ordinary man or woman in the street. The nuns who were her tutors passed on her abilities and the offer of a position in a 'Government department' was put to her. She was highly educated and ideal for the standards expected of Intelligence. Her life revolved around her job. She never married and only an odd occasions was seen in the company of men. She was a theatre-goer and loved classical music, always attending the shows with her aging mother. She had never wanted for anything; her parents were wealthy, but she had disappointed them by never marrying. She was forty-seven, and still a good-looking woman.

Jeremy Warburton, her colleague, at fifty-eight the eldest employee, had also spent all his working life in Intelligence. He'd been conscripted at the start of the war but his constant questioning of the workings of military procedures soon earned him attention. Intelligence needed people who could pry into details and it wasn't long before SIS used his services. He proved invaluable throughout and after the war, staying on until the mid-fifties when he was transferred to the Vicar's department. Jeremy, Balquidder knew, was a stickler for detail. He could never be happy unless everything was compiled exactly as procedure demanded. Often he and Pat Birdsall rechecked the details on sheets to make doubly sure procedure was being followed.

It took two hours to complete the reconstruction of the previous Thursday, but nothing transpired. Everything went as normal, not a thing out of place. It seemed impossible that anything had slipped through. They began again. Two hours was the allotted time for the sheets to be completed, the rest of the working day being taken up with other duties.

They began again. Substitute paperwork was circulated, clocks were turned back and the staff gathered in the corridor with their street clothes on. Keeping to the same order as before they entered the office, bade their good wishes and took their seats. Eleanor Greenhill put on the kettle for tea and joked with Warburton, Marjorie Atkinson asked everybody their opinion of a TV show and Johnnie Trench debated the prospects of Arsenal.

Balquidder watched each one in turn for a few seconds at a time, his eyes moving swiftly from one to the other, looking for the slightest thing out of place. Two hours passed and nothing happened. He ordered a re-run.

The third try looked as though it would produce another negative result, but when it, was nearly over he detected a change in Pat Birdsall. Her normal efficient manner had slipped for an instant. Warburton's hand had been out ready to take a pile of sheets from her and she'd pushed them into his hand rather than place them. Warburton looked up in that brief instant, but possibly putting it down to frustration went back to what he was doing. Balquidder didn't let it pass.

She was edgy. Unlike her. He let the exercise finish and ordered them to start again, this time watching Birdsall all the way through. She became more edgy, agitated, once or twice twisting her head quickly to see if he were watching her. Something was on her mind.

When the exercise was reaching its conclusion it appeared that nothing was going to come of it. No one put a foot wrong, but Pat Birdsall was becoming more and more agitated and he was convinced that she had remembered something. Suddenly Warburton stopped. Pat Birdsall was handing him two piles of sheets. That was wrong. Only one pile of sheets was to be held by a person at any time. Warburton whispered to her, prompting her memory. She dropped both piles on the floor and covered her face with her hands.

'I've only just remembered it,' said Warburton. 'Pat dropped them that morning.'

Balquidder nodded and got to his knees. The two piles were 'RIP' and 'V' sheets. They had fallen practically intact except that the sheet at the bottom of the 'V' pile had somehow found its way between the two piles.

'Carry on from there.' Balquidder said.

Warburton bent over. He didn't get off his chair, but leaned, off-balance, and scooped up the two piles. The 'V' sheet could easily have been pulled to the bottom of the wrong pile.

'Did you check them when you took them off the floor?'

'Now that I remember, no.'

'Did you check them off on the VDU before they were prepared for dispatch and shredding?'

Warburton reddened. 'We did, but I don't know—'

Balquidder accepted that the cause was found. But the pair had committed an unforgivable sin. They should have spotted the mistake when checking-off. They most probably checked them off by habit, assuming that everything was in order.

He ordered another re-run to make sure. Again no one put a foot wrong except at the end when the piles were dropped. That had to be it. Anyway, to look for something else could take a year. The error could not be undone, however, and bawling them out would serve no purpose, but both knew they would never achieve any further promotion within the department. There was no need to say anything.

Why, though, Balquidder wondered, had Pat Birdsall made the first mistake? Had she done her job properly it wouldn't have happened. If she had had her mind on the job it wouldn't have happened. So if her mind wasn't fully occupied with the job she had to have been thinking about something else, and that something else was significant enough to let her mind stray. And that meant that it would be something he should have been told about.

To triple-check, Balquidder had Pat Birdsall programme an entry for the 'V' section of the computer to display possible omissions. The VDU showed that it had been entered but not checked-off, and worse, nor had another.

Balquidder nearly fainted. It was disastrous that one sheet should become misplaced, but two! There was no term to describe the damage that could have been caused. Balquidder trembled. There was no way they could go back seven years to find how it had slipped through.

He all but flew through to his own office and again called the Vicar. The Vicar was far from pleased.

'... But it's too late to do anything about it,' he added. 'What we must do is make sure Washington doesn't dig too deeply.'

Balquidder put down his special receiver and began to think. Only the CIA could have the sheet. They had to have it, which meant that Rogal knew when he paid his visit earlier.

26

Damn the Government cuts! thought Balquidder. Cutting down on staff was all right in some of the industrial concerns, but having cuts introduced into the security services was downright diabolical. How did they expect the department to run efficiently if there were insufficient people to run it? If they had the numbers they asked for the 'RIP' sheets would be handled by a single section, and they'd never have come into contact with the Vicar's work.

And yet it was something he couldn't complain about. Who could he complain to? He was one of only three people who had contact with the Vicar, and he hadn't even met him. Only two men ever had, and one of those was dead. The other lived in Russia. The Vicar had always been a spy, and it was in Berlin during the last days of May 1945 when he really came into his own.

Four

Berlin was a shambles. Incessant Allied raids, day and night, had reduced the city to a ruin. Refugees fleeing from Russian troops flooded the streets, on their way to freedom in the Allied sectors. The Western Allies felt sorry for the refugees. The Russians were treating everyone as a potential Hitler. Men and boys were shot down without mercy whether they were in uniform or not, or were taken forcible away and never seen again; women of any age and condition were raped and murdered.

But the Western Allies could do nothing to help. It was forbidden to have any contact with the defeated enemy, unless the enemy was being questioned on the whereabouts of wanted criminals. They could only stand back and watch helplessly.

An armistice was signed and the war ended officially, but three weeks after the signing the Russians were still advancing. It was only a matter of time before the Western Allies would have to relinquish some of the territory they had won.

It came, and with it friction between the armies of the West and those from the East. The West had lost many men and women in the long conflict and desired only peace, while the armies of the East, who had lost some twenty million, wanted revenge. Russian troops strutted around Berlin and the Eastern half of Germany and continually issued orders, orders that other allies were expected to respect.

The hunt for war-criminals went on by East and West, and Russian troops thought nothing of smashing open an Allied lock-up to drag out a terrified German, whom they immediately shot. Allied soldiers, already sickened by the long war, had no stomach for a fight, and nine times out of ten gave

28

in to Russian demands.

Spies were everywhere. Russian, American, British and Nazi. All were on the look-out for someone or another. Among them was a 37-year old army chaplain named Phillip Huntingdon.

Huntingdon was attached to the Secret Intelligence Service and, in the guise of a chaplain searching for lost or deserted British soldiers, he gathered all the information he could about his Eastern allies. He wore khaki like everyone else, and a peaked cap, but it was impossible for anyone to miss his black clergyman's shirt and white dog-collar. The purple cloth that hung around his neck made him stand out like a sore thumb.

The Russians steered clear off him. They knew he was a religious man of some kind. They would have shot him if he had been German, but he was the kind of ally they could not afford to shoot. The NKVD had issued specific instructions that no religious men attached to the Allies were to be harmed, so long as they were British or American – Poles didn't count – for too much trouble would be caused and Russia could find herself fighting another war. But the NKVD also issued other instructions. Anyone discovered or reported speaking to one of these men would be shot as a spy.

It suited Huntingdon. He wanted a clear field, yet the Russians hindered him in other ways. In their eagerness to rid their sector of him, they regularly handed over British soldiers who had lost their way in the severe fighting.

Huntingdon plodded on, fetching a piece of information here and there about Russian strengths and aims, and counting the number of obviously NKVD men and women who drove madly from one sector to another.

It was dark when he first met Kocker. Russian troops were staggering through a flattened area of Berlin drunk on vodka. He stood in the shadows of the remnants of a building until they passed, then stepped out to follow them to their destination. He was stopped by another shadow.

'Good evening, my friend.' The shadow said, speaking Russian.

Huntingdon stopped and automatically moved his hand to the thick bible tucked in his battledress jacket.

'There is no need for the gun, my friend.' said the shadow. 'I have come to help you.'

Huntingdon said nothing. He could see the stranger, nor was he going to open his mouth until he knew who it was.

'You are the Holy Man. We watch you.'

Still Huntingdon said nothing.

'You do not trust me, my friend. No matter. Return here tomorrow night if you think you can trust me by then. In the meantime, think on this. Those men you saw just now. They have been ordered to attack your lock-up in the Viennastrasse and remove your prisoners. Anyone who resists them is to be shot. I give you information, my friend. Think on it, and use it if you can. If you think you can trust me, return at the same time tomorrow night.'

The shadow moved back and disappeared into the night.

Huntingdon mopped his brow. He hadn't noticed he'd been sweating. But he was now and it was running into his eyes. How on earth had the shadow known that he could understand and speak Russian?

He couldn't treat the warning lightly. Gathering his wits he hurried, via ruined buildings, to the Viennastrasse.

He did not approach the lock-up to inform the sentries on duty about the warning he'd been given, but stood some way off to watch if anything would happen.

. It was nearly an hour before the Russians came, more drunk than ever. Fifteen of them armed with ugly looking machine-guns. One of them threw a grenade into the lock-up, an explosion followed and the entire group charged inside, firing their guns. The occupants defended themselves fiercely. Four Russians came staggering out doubled up in pain and flopped to the ground. A civilian in shirt-sleeves came running out with part of his face blown away, firing a revolver. A drunken Russian followed him and cut him in two with a long burst.

It was soon over. The firing stopped and immediately afterwards screams came from the lock-up. The screaming increased and suddenly seven men in German uniforms were thrown into the street. The Russians came after them, beating and kicking, using guns and knives, anything that came to hand, and before long the German prisoners were unconscious.

30

It was only then that the Russians shot them.

Huntingdon kept still. He knew that if he moved he was a dead man, yet he was drawn by the sight. It amazed him that a Russian had actually warned him that it would happen. But it didn't mean that he trusted the Russian — that's if he were a Russian. The NKVD, he knew, had no remorse in using a hundred lives to achieve very little. He could be set up for something.

He returned to the place the next night without reporting the incident. There had been similar occurrences all over Berlin and sooner or later the occupational authorities would remove suspects to a safer location as soon as they were picked up. He could never say how he came across the information.

The shadow was there, waiting for him.

'Good evening, my friend.'

'Wotcha, cock,' Huntingdon returned.

'Kock?' The shadow was taken by surprise. The expression was something he didn't understand.

Huntingdon waved a hand. 'It's a term we use in London when we greet a friend.'

'We are friends?' The shadow asked with some satisfaction.

'Maybe.'

'Maybe? Did I not give you useful information?'

'Useful? Yes, but to what end? What do you want in return?'

'I want nothing, my friend. You still do not trust me, perhaps?'

'Perhaps,' nodded Huntingdon.

'Then I will make you trust me. Listen, my government has no intention of giving up any of the territory it has liberated. Tell that to your superiors. They will understand ... I will tell you something else: tomorrow, the so-called leader of the Christian-Democrat Party in the Russian sector will be killed. I do not jest, nor do I wish to trap you ... you see, I know what is behind your collar. Come back tomorrow night and I will have more ...'

Huntingdon let him go. The prospect excited him. The Russian could be genuine, he thought. But time would tell.

Huntingdon turned up at the appointed time again the next night, and again the shadow was there.

'Watcher, Kocker!' The shadow greeted him. Huntingdon smiled in the darkness.

'What have you found out today, my friend?' The shadow asked.

'The Russians announced today,' Huntingdon replied, 'that Willhelm Kusch was shot while attempting to escape from the police.'

'As I told you it would happen, my friend.'

'Yes,' Huntingdon conceded. 'You did.'

Huntingdon had waited most of the day for the report. It came at two minutes after five in the afternoon. A Russian despatch-rider drove up to an Allied check-point and handed over a communiqué. The message told the Allies they need not search further for one Willhelm Kusch, proven war-criminal. Kusch had been captured that day by local police but escaped shortly after, stealing a firearm in the process. Chased by local police he had discharged the stolen firearm and, having no alternative, his pursuers had to shoot him.

The Allied war-crimes commission could only shake its head. Willhelm Kusch was a minor political figure, but the only figure left in the Easter sector of Berlin capable of forming a government body. He certainly was no war criminal. Similar ends had come to other people involved in politics, all anti-communist.

'I have a fire alight nearby,' said the shadow. 'Perhaps we could sit by it and keep warm.'

Huntingdon said nothing and followed.

There was a large fire burning in the ruins of a building and around it were several men. The shadow grunted at them and they moved away, taking up positions further into the shadows.

'They are my men,' the shadow said. 'They will make sure we are not disturbed. Please sit down.'

They sat on lumps of wood. A dirty saucepan was on top of the fire boiling the life out of pure coffee. Huntingdon studied the man in the light.

The Russian was in his mid-forties. His face was thin and

tired, his eyes sunk well into his head and most of his teeth were missing. He was tall, nearly 6 ft; his hair was cropped to the skull, where recent scars were visible.

Huntingdon knew he had to be NKVD, and it intrigued him that the Russian should supply him with advanced information. But there would be a reason. He prayed that it would be the right reason.

'Would you like some American coffee?' Kocker asked.

'Please.' Huntingdon didn't particularly want the coffee, but a chill was coming into the night and anything hot would do him no harm.

'You are wondering, my friend?'

Huntingdon nodded.

'What do they call you in England? A priest?'

'No, that is Roman Catholic. I am referred to as a Vicar.'

'I know,' said Kocker.

'Indeed?' They were fencing.

'I must know that I can trust you, my Vicar.'

Huntingdon nodded his acknowledgement.

'You did not pass on the information I gave you, Vicar.' The Russian sipped the scalding hot coffee straight from the old saucepan.

'I had my men follow you to watch what you did.'

Again Huntingdon nodded.

'I could be important to you, Vicar, could I not?'

'Very much so, Cock.'

'Kocker and Vicar, eh?'

'If you like.'

'My reasons?' Kocker looked over the top of the saucepan.

Huntingdon shrugged.

A packet of Russian cigarettes was produced and shared. Huntingdon grimaced at the taste.

'Russia is decimated, Vicar. We have won a violent war, but it does not end there. Already our armies are being taken back home, and none of them will ever see their families again. Why? Because they have seen the West. They have seen the fine houses even the lowliest peasants live in; they have seen how well fed the Allied armies are ... They have seen too much. Were they to tell about what they had seen there would

33

be a revolution ...'

Huntingdon knew what Kocker meant. Every Allied soldier in Germany who had come into contact with Russians had been amazed at some of their antics. Many of the Russians had never seen running water or electricity. They spent hours turning on and off taps, switching on and off lights, and often they ripped out the taps and switches to take home, believing they would work like magic. They had avidly gathered up an Allied newspaper or magazine to gaze with wonder at the coloured adverts. It astounded them that even Germany could still have such things while they, the victors, had nothing.

. 'Do you realise what will happen now, Vicar? Once again we will become prisoners in our own country. It will become a treasonable offence to speak of anything in the West. Did you know that my people did not know there were radio sets that can pick up foreign broadcasts? In Russia programmes are fed by wire to receivers. We hear only what our leader wants us to hear.'

Huntingdon knew. He had kept his eyes and ears open. It was the earnest desire of the security services to learn everything they could about Russia and her intentions before a barrier was set up between them. But he said nothing. He wanted Kocker to say it all.

'We will become slaves once more, Vicar.'

'You could leave.'

'And be murdered? I know too much, Vicar.'

'What are you? A colonel?'

Kocker nodded. 'A colonel of a military division, Vicar. We have fought from Stalingrad to Berlin. Most of my men are dead, killed by the Nazis or taken away by the political directorate. I am still alive because of my position in the Party and the directorate.'

'Why would you be murdered if you leave?'

'Take my warning, Vicar. There will be murders soon. We have taken over many countries, and as I've already warned you, my government will never give them up. These countries have their own political leaders, but they are an obstacle to Moscow: Moscow will remove them. A team of men is already in the West seeking out a Ukrainian nationalist. They will kill him no matter how long it takes. And plans are being drawn up to have Jan Masaryk killed in the future. No, my vicar, it does not pay to desert Mother Russia.'

Huntingdon knew of Masaryk, and that troubled him. Thomas Masaryk was the founder and first President of Czechoslovakia, and his son Jan had been a representative for his government in London before the war. Murdering someone like Masaryk would be a disaster for the Czechs, and if it was true it showed the lengths to which Stalin would go to dominate Eastern Europe.

'It worries you?' Huntingdon asked.

'It worries many of us, Vicar. You do not know Russia. If I were seen speaking to you I would be shot without trial. Any Westerner, especially priests, are considered spies and a dangerous influence. Have you not noticed that there is no longer a comradely relationship between your troops and ours?'

It was very noticeable, thought Huntingdon. It was so noticeable that one could gain the impression that the Allies had fought the wrong enemy. More and more the Russians were forcing the Allies out of their sector at the point of a gun.

'We did not fight for this, Vicar.'

'And why do you tell me?'

'Because you are a spy, Mr Philip Huntingdon ... my vicar. There is much we know about your department in the SIS. You see, we also have our spies. I do not know their names, but they are like woodworm in all your security departments. I have known about you since the first day you arrived. I have had you followed every minute of every day to see whom you spoke to and what you did. I believe you are the man I want?'

'For what?'

'There is a way I can get back at the men who have turned our country into a giant slave market. I cannot leave, or they would hunt me down, and my family, too, will be killed.'

'Are you proposing to become a traitor, Kocker?'

'Not a traitor, Vicar, but a patriot. The few rule the many in Russia and the few live well. I am one of them. I will live well when I return eventually. My family will want for nothing, but there are millions of others who will suffer. Perhaps in my own way I can help to relieve some of that suffering. Would you say that was treason?'

'How do you propose to accomplish that?' Huntingdon ignored the question.

'By sending you secret information, Vicar.'

'Oh?' Huntingdon tried not to appear excited. 'How?'

'I will find a way.'

'How will your men feel about that?'

'They do not know.'

'One of them will report our meeting.'

'None of them will live to tell what they know.'

'You'll kill them?'

Kocker nodded.

'I will have to speak to someone first.' Huntingdon said.

'Churchill?'

'No.'

'A pity. He is a shrewd man, your Mr Churchill. He is feared and hated in Russia.'

'How can I contact you if I have anything to tell you?'

'I will contact you, Vicar. I will be in Berlin for some time and I will know when you come again. You see, I have the task of creating the secret police in the Eastern sector of Berlin.'

'Then perhaps we'll meet again, Kocker.'

'We will.'

'Until then ...'

'You do not wish to know my name?'

'Oh,' Huntingdon said mildly. 'I know who you are.'

Kocker smiled, the gaps between his teeth showing up. 'You are also a shrewd man, Vicar. Okay, we do not need our names. You will hear from me as Kocker.'

Five

Rogal left Balquidder in a fury. Although the Englishman had been plausible enough to be believed he knew it had been all lies. London had made a foul-up and was trying to cover by denying it. But what was more hurtful was the fact that London had someone deep inside the Kremlin and hadn't told the agency. That was unforgiveable.

But two could play at the same game. London exploited the Agency with their man, and the Agency was expert at exploiting others. He could play dirty too.

From the embassy he made several telephone calls, issued instructions to various agency employees in London and took a taxi to Waterloo Station. At the station he approached a newspaper seller and bought one of the early editions of the evenings. On paying he handed the seller a pound note, folded in a certain way. The man took the note, unfolded it swiftly with one hand, read the message on it and thrust it into his pocket, all in a single innocent action.

Rogal wasted an hour wandering among the station concourse then went on to a restaurant in the West End and asked if a table was booked in the name of Jennings. A waiter nodded and showed him to a screened-off table where another man sat. Rogal joined him, gestured for silence until the waiter had gone and said:

'I need your help, Boris.'

Boris Petrokovic, a 'Cultural' attaché at the Russian Embassy smiled. Why else would he have received a telephone call from Waterloo Station?

'Were you followed?' Rogal went on.

'I am never followed, my friend.' Petrokovic said. 'I am

trusted, remember.'

Rogal was blunt and to the point. 'Could there be a British spy in Moscow?'

'Undoubtedly.'

'I mean, high up.'

'How high?'

'Very high.' Regal couldn't give too much away.

'Political or military?'

'Political.'

'It's improbable.'

'Why improbable?'

'You should know, my friend. Anyone of any consequence in Moscow is old. They are of the old school and are untouchable as spies. That is why they are chosen.'

Rogal knew that. It was unlikely that anyone inside the Soviet Government was under sixty. Older men were unlikely to be spies. They wanted to finish their terms in office and retire in comparative comfort. There was too much at stake. It was the younger ones who risked their lives to spy for the West.

'Could it be remotely possible?'

'Everything is possible.'

'What is your opinion?'

'I would very much doubt it ... Why, is there some trouble?'

'Nothing we can't handle, but we'd like to get some information without London knowing.'

'London knows things, then?'

'We think London has someone in Moscow we don't know about. We would like to know who he is.'

'Yesss ...'

Rogal didn't mention that the Agency also had a spy tucked away.

'Will you see what you can find out, Boris?'

'It will be difficult, but I will try my best. Give me a week.'

'Too long.'

'As soon as I can then.'

'I'd be grateful.'

Rogal was proud of his achievements with Petrokovic. Two years earlier he'd turned him round in Paris. It had been difficult. Petrokovic had been stubborn, afraid even, but when

38

certain negatives were shown to him he caved in. He was a wealth of information. Only Rogal knew about him, but it was a disappointing day when the Paris embassy had transferred Petrokovic to London. Still, it had worked out right.

Unknown to Rogal, Petrokovic was no traitor. An hour after their meeting he was sitting facing the KGB director, resident in Great Britain.

'The Allies have a spy somewhere high in Moscow, Comrade Director, and the Americans are worried. Principally, from what I could gather, he is in the pay of the British, but his information has recently not been shared between the two in accordance with the RIP agreement.'

'Did he mention the RIP agreement?'

'He has told me about it in the past, when we were in Paris, but not today.'

'Are his movements being checked?'

'Yes. We had a man waiting when he arrived in London. He has already paid Balquidder a visit.'

'I would like to have listened in on that meeting.'

'We have tried to infiltrate that area, Comrade Director, but we are always found out. We have never been able to reason why.'

'I know, I know. The British have methods I would pay well to get hold of.'

'What shall I tell him?'

'Stall him. Try to get him to give you more information to work on. Perhaps then we might ourselves find a spy. Nonetheless, I shall inform Moscow.'

Patricia Birdsall knew should would have to tell Balquidder. She couldn't do so before because she was embarrassed. The only time she'd been with men was when they'd invited her to theatres or concerts. Perhaps they'd have a meal and a drink beforehand, but afterwards she always made certain they dropped her at the entrance to the block of flats she lived in. She'd been terrified of inviting them in.

Having a husband hadn't bothered her in her twenties and thirties, she'd been too interested in her work, but when she reached the forty mark her attitude altered. Her mother helped light the fires. She was still a beautiful woman, her mother had said. She could still find a husband and live happily.

The more the idea played on her mind the more she liked it, but she didn't know how. As a convent schoolgirl meeting members of the opposite sex was strictly forbidden; it was ingrained in them, and when joining the department she was discouraged from making too many male friends.

She'd been able to carry on as usual. No one suspected that she would like to have a husband. They assumed she was prepared to spend the rest of her life as a spinster; they never realised how she'd ached. For seven years she'd suffered the pangs of emotion, but she remained a virgin – until David Noble came into her life.

David was ten years her junior. They'd met six months before at a concert at the Albert Hall. They'd got chatting and before she knew what she was doing she'd accepted his invitation to dine another evening.

David was a gentleman. He treated her with respect and kindness that evening. And she'd bought new clothes for the occasion; she'd taken great care with her hair and face – she'd felt like a teenager getting ready for her first date.

It was a wonderful evening. David kept by her side all evening, gently holding her hand and saying the right kind of things. He's taken her home, kissing her hand on the doorstep, getting her to promise they would dine again.

How she'd wanted to go into work the next day and tell everyone about her man. She could have sat all day and talked about him, but it would have embarrassed her. She was forty-seven and the thought of the others maybe laughing at her put her off. It stayed bottled up inside her, and she knew full well that it was against the rules. Balquidder should have been told immediately; David should have been investigated, but she couldn't do it. For the first time in her life she was in love and she didn't want it spoiled.

They first made love four months after they met. She'd been both excited and petrified. No man had as much as seen her petticoat, but shaking, with goose-pimples covering her, she'd allowed him to undress her. It was unbelievable. A little painful at first, but the pain soon went, to be substituted for spasms of ecstasy.

She remembered the day when the mistake was made. Reliving the events of the previous evening her thoughts were entirely about David. They'd been making love for two months, and always the next day she felt wonderful, dreaming about him and wishing their next meeting was that night.

Now she was worried. Balquidder knew she had something on her mind. He would be cross; he would bawl her out — although he wouldn't do it in front of the others — but once he met David he would soften. She had broken the rules and would lose her seniority, but it wouldn't be so bad when they were married. The position wouldn't matter then.

They were naked on Patricia's bed. He had done things to her with his lips and tongue that made her body scream for more. She wished it could go on for ever.

'Would you like a drink, my lovely?' He said, running his tongue across her swollen nipples. She nodded, smiling, and thought about Balquidder. She would tell him tomorrow.

She wasn't supposed to drink too often. They'd had two or three during the course of the evening, more than she normally had, but it was wonderful being with David and she didn't care.

It was gin, and even with tonic in it, it tasted funny.

'Does your drink taste funny, darling?' She asked.

He shook his head, downing his quickly. 'It was perfect, my lovely … Just like you.'

They made love again, slowly and quietly. Patricia closed her eyes with bliss.

It was too short and she wanted more but sleep was reaching her.

'You're tired.' He said.

'A little …'

She could hardly keep her eyes open. The room was spinning and David was appearing and vanishing.

'Tell me about your work, my lovely …'

'I'm only a typist …' She murmured.

He studied her. Under her flickering eyelids her eyes rolled. She was ready.

'Does Mr Balquidder work you hard?'

She stirred at the mention of Balquidder's name.

'Is he your only superior?'

'Mmm ...'

'What about "V"?'

'Mmm?'

' "V", my lovely. Who is "V"?'

She was afraid now. The urge to sleep was still there, but fear was holding it back. This wasn't right. It wasn't supposed to happen this way.

' "V", my lovely!' He lifted her head roughly. 'Who is "V"?'

Her head rolled to one side and he grabbed her hair, shouting at her, then screaming.

'Who is "V"?'

She didn't reply. She was out. Gone ... God-damn it! He'd told them she wasn't ready. It was too soon. In time she would have told him of her own accord. And the drug was no good. She was supposed to talk, not go to sleep. He lifted her eyelids and peered behind them. He swore.

'Silly cow!'

He dressed quickly and made for the door, turned back and tried to get her awake, but she was dead to the world. He left, swearing to himself.

Patricia sat up when he'd gone and began to cry. How she'd managed to keep the flow from coming was a miracle, but they came now, shiny and wet. The mention of Balquidder had spoiled it. She couldn't go on after that and playing doggo seemed the only thing to do.

It had all been too good to be true ... How could she ever have hoped for someone's love? ... It was stupid ... She shouldn't have allowed herself to be taken like that ... She was nothing but a silly old woman.

She walked unsteadily to the telephone. As she picked up the receiver she looked back at the bed. She had enjoyed herself. She'd never experienced anything like it. But it would have to be a memory.

She dialled Balquidder's number; he would be understanding. While she waited she tweaked her nipples.

42

Six

Tony Gillet didn't know anything about it. One second he was walking quietly along Gloucester Road and the next he was in a dark pit. When he came to he was in the back seat of a car. His head throbbed with pain, and he could feel dried blood cracking at the back of his neck. He could see the back of the driver, a wide-set man; another was in the front passenger seat pointing a gun at his forehead, and two others, holding him firmly in the 'whore's grip', were on either side of him. He said nothing. He knew who they were.

'Hi, Tony!' The man with the gun said.

Gillet smiled weakly. It was his old friend Donny Swenson. They'd worked together on joint projects.

'You're among friends,' said Swenson.

Gillet said nothing.

'An international conference, one might say,' Swenson smiled. 'You know — where we get together and discuss items of mutual interest.'

Gillet raised his eyebrows but still said nothing.

'It's for all our benefits, I assure you.'

Without having to turn, Gillet knew where they were going. They were headed west on the M4, but he knew of no American safe houses out there.

'Who is "V", Tony?'

'Who?' Gillet couldn't help replying. The question was unexpected.

' "V", someone in your organisation who goes under the simple code-name of "V". We would like to know who he is.'

'Never heard of him.'

The grips of his upper arms grew tighter.

'I tell you, I've never heard of him.'

'You're a liar, Tony.' The gun cracked across his forehead, the sight cutting deep into his flesh.

The car drove non-stop to a secluded house on the outskirts of Slough, which, Gillet thought, was careless of his American colleagues. Now that he knew they would be forced to abandon it.

The tight grip on his arms never faltered when he climbed from the car, nor did the gun waver from his forehead. He was firmly taken into the house and into a bare room. The men followed and a fifth brought a chair for him to sit on. When he had, manacles were fastened to his wrists and to the arms of the chair. The fifth man he knew as Rogal, a big noise in the CIA.

'Pleased to meet you, Tony,' said Rogal, smiling.

Gillet nodded slightly.

'We won't fuck about, Tony. Indiscretions is the reason we're here. Your Mr Balquidder has been somewhat indiscreet about certain information. He has access to certain parts of Moscow that he hasn't told us about, and about which we want to know. I don't expect you to know everything, but there must be something you can tell us. Now, Tony, you can tell us in one of two ways. You can either tell us straight off and walk out of here in one piece, or we will break bones in your body until you do. And then you'll have to satisfy us that you've told us everything you know. Which will it be?'

'I don't know what the hell you're talking about, mate.'

Rogal nodded and one of the men shot off Gillet's right thumb. Gillet fainted.

When he came round blood was pouring from the stump. No one had made any attempt to stop it.

'Well?' He heard Rogal's voice.

'I don't know what you're talking about.'

His left thumb was shot off.

And it went on. One by one his fingers were shot off. The questions kept coming, questions about 'V' and a man in Moscow. They started on his toes; one from the left foot and one from the right. He screamed for mercy, appealing to them that he couldn't reply to their questions. When he had two toes left he'd no more energy left to scream.

'We'll get you a doctor, Tony, if you tell us something.'

'Don't you understand?' Gillet managed to whisper. 'I don't know.' Tears, the fear of death, ran down his cheeks.

'No guy would be that patriotic,' Swenson said.

'I guess not,' Rogal said. He nodded. Swenson shot Gillet through the head. Gillet had told the truth.

Seven

Balquidder was furious with both himself and Patricia Birdsall. A check on the previous month's appraisal form had shown that she was having an affair with a younger man. He had immediately assigned a male and female couple to tail her and report on her further before confronting her with the breach of regulations. That had been a mistake. To his regret he realised that he should have interviewed her right away. He made a mental note to have appraisals done on a two-weekly basis instead of monthly.

'Why?' He asked.

Patricia had a housecoat on and was still crying.

'He was so nice ... He said so many things to me that sounded just right ... I believed him ... I wanted to believe him ... I wanted him and I loved him ... I thought that when we announced our wedding it would be all right ... It was too late when I realised ...'

Balquidder hushed her. 'It's too late to go back. What's done is done. We have to make sure it doesn't happen again.'

'It won't, I promise you.' Patricia made up her mind never to trust a man again.

'Have you had much to drink?'

'A little more than usual.'

'All right. I'm going to give you a sleeping powder. It'll knock you out for at least twelve hours. When you wake I want you to take another, which I will leave out for you, but eat a meal in between. Come back to the office the day after tomorrow as if nothing has happened. Do you understand?'

Patricia nodded, sniffling.

'I don't want any others on my staff wondering what's

wrong. I'll tell them tomorrow that you've caught a chill ... but you must be back the next day as if nothing has happened ...'
He took her hand. 'Can you manage that? It's most important that you do.'

'Yes, sir.'

'All right, then. Take this ...'

Balquidder emptied a white powder into a glass of water and gave it to her.

'It tastes of peppermint to disguise the taste.'

Patricia drank it down and Balquidder placed a small sachet of the powder on the table.

'Into bed, now. I'll stay with you until you're asleep.'

'Thank you, sir. You've been kind and understanding.'

'It's my job.' Balquidder muttered and went out of the bedroom.

He waited ten minutes, staring out of a window across the roofs of London, then returned to the bedroom. Patricia's face was deep into the pillow and her hair was loose, giving her an enticing appearance. He turned her over and listened to her heart. She was dead. He picked up the other sachet of powder and went to the telephone.

Balquidder stayed on his feet all night, then changed his clothing before journeying to the American embassy in Grosvenor Square. He presented his diplomatic pass to the pretty receptionist and asked for Rogal.

'Mr Rogal will not be in today, sir.'

'I'll wait,' said Balquidder. 'Get him!'·

'Yes, sir.'

Balquidder's diplomatic pass was green, ensuring that holders of green passes were given immediate assistance by friendly nations. The girl would find Rogal.

He took a seat from where he could watch the entrance, his bowler hat on his lap and his brolly standing alongside his right knee, as if to attention.

Thirty minutes went by and the receptionist approached him. There was a telephone call for him. He could take it in one of the public booths.

What he heard surprised and angered him. The voice on

47

the other end, instantly recogniseable, told him about Tony Gillet.

'Thank you, sir,' he said and went back to sit down.

Rogal arrived after two hours and came straight to him.

'You wanted to see me?'

'Yes,' Balquidder nodded once. 'Somewhere private.'

'I have an office ...'

'I know a small pub.'

'Your choice, Colin.'

'Thank you.' Balquidder rose and put on his bowler hat.

Going down the steps in front of the embassy Balquidder began to speak, staring straight ahead.

'You could find yourself unwelcome in Britain, old chap, if you don't make an effort to mend your ways.'

'How do you mean?' Rogal was ready. He knew what was coming.

'I'm talking about the murders of two of my staff – one of them most brutal.'

'Two?' Rogal was shaken. He'd been prepared to deny one. Two had put him off-stride.

'Yes, old chap,' Balquidder's brolly swung in time to his regimental step. 'A fine young man, Anthony Gillet; he had good potential ... You were responsible for that, old dear, and right across my own doorstep. And Miss Patricia Birdsall, one of my long-serving clerks, was poisoned last night. I won't have my—'

'Hang on!' Rogal pulled Balquidder to a halt. 'What the hell's this about poison?'

'A handsome young gigolo-type? Goes by the name of David Noble? Real name Edward Anderson? Surely you're not attempting naivety?'

'Now look! I don't know anything about any poisoning!'

'Now you look, old dear,' Balquidder continued his march and Rogal ran after him to catch up. 'If you persist in knocking-off my employees you may find yourself involved in a bereavement.' Balquidder suddenly stopped and faced Rogal, letting his warning sink in.

'Hey, are you threatening me?'

'Certainly not, old dear ...' Balquidder began marching again, and again Rogal had to run after him. 'Below our dignity to threaten one. I'm relaying you a fact. Persist in poking the old hooter where it doesn't belong and your family might find itself living off the Agency's death benefit fund ... I should feel sorry for them, myself. Lovely children ...'

Balquidder doffed his hat, pointed his brolly in the air, and smiled.

'Good morrow, old chap.'

Rogal stood rooted to the spot and spat with anger. He hadn't realised it until too late. The God-damned Englishman had made him look small. He'd actually ran after him to make a denial ... Shit! The john-faced Limey had had him running like a schoolboy who'd been caught pissing against a wall. The cunning bastard!

Balquidder went into a quiet pub for a drink and to think. The situation was serious-plus. The CIA had been quick off the mark. Gillet was unfortunate, but Birdsall was necessary. They'd got to her once and they could have got to her again. It had been going on longer than he realised – six whole months! He was lacking in his own security; he should have had Noble tagged from the first day. It shook him realising that his own security was bad. His area could never afford mistakes, not when the Vicar was involved ... Even he didn't want to know where the Vicar got his information from.

But the Americans would never give up until they found a way in. They would spend millions of dollars just to get a foothold. They'd been trying to get in, that was evident with Birdsall; they'd try harder. But if by some fluke they did manage it – and it was a mighty big 'if' – they'd come unstuck. He knew the Vicar's methods. The Vicar would simply have his contact killed. Still, he mused, it did give one a certain feeling of satisfaction to know that Washington was pooping itself with worry.

But it was serious sure enough. The blasted Americans would cause so much trouble that the Russians would guess something was wrong, then they would get in on the act. The Americans were bad sports sometimes.

That didn't solve anything, though, he prompted himself.

The department had been on to a good thing and it was something they couldn't afford to lose. At all costs they would have to protect the Vicar and his man.

There would have to be some diversionary tactics.

Eight

The situation in Berlin deteriorated. Bands of communists roamed the ruined streets of the city shooting anyone who had in any way supported the Nazi regime or the old republic. Old political leaders, no lovers of Hitler, were taken to Moscow, tried by the 'people's courts' and sentenced to death; and at the Brandenburg Gate Russian rifles began to be pointed at the West.

Huntingdon went back to London and reported the contact he had made. He did not mention his contact's name, nor was it asked of him, but he suggested that the gift of a lifetime had fallen into their lap.

Events were swift. Huntingdon's superior contacted the heads of other security departments and a secret meeting was held. Even without Kocker's name they learned enough to know that he was well-placed. They appreciated the need for a contact to be protected, only his controller knowing his true identity, and agreed that he would be an asset.

Huntingdon would be immediately removed from the SIS and set up his own department. The directors of the main security departments would be given a telephone number to ring and information would be exchanged when necessary. All services would supply him with any information he required, on demand, and would allot part of their annual budget to finance the new department. How he spent the money would entirely be his affair. No one would know his identity and this, they reasoned, would safeguard the identity of the man in Moscow.

Huntingdon would develop the contact. Periodically he would pass information on to Moscow, genuine and damaging information, sufficient to have the man recognised as a force within the Soviet Government, from which he would gain promotion to higher levels. Then he would be most useful. It would take time, many years, but in the end Britain would be all the more secure with first-hand knowledge, for they were in no doubt that Moscow had similar people in their own government.

. It gave Huntingdon a clear field. Secure in his own small department any Russian spies in the government would never learn of Kocker's existence. He could work at his own pace, a faceless individual, and pip others long before the finishing post. He went back to Germany, for months taking the guise of a minor official with the Ministry of Education, handing out documents to displaced Europeans who had been granted permission to reside in Britain. It suited him splendidly. Being a linguist he could converse with most of them and when he handed out and explained his documents he was able to learn things.

Often he picked up valuable tit-bits of information and was able to see through some of the 'refugees'. There were spies among them, from every country liberated by Russian forces. From the few but hidden questions he asked, he was able to pinpoint those who were not bona-fide. The information he passed on, and the Russian NKVD became extremely angry at the results.

He had been in Berlin for five weeks before Kocker made contact again. Like the first time it was totally unexpected.

'Hello, my Vicar.'

The voice startled him, but it was a pleasure to hear it. It was dark and there were few street lights on, but he could see nothing. He stopped and fiddled with his shoelaces and waited for Kocker to speak again.

'To your right, Vicar.'

He turned at right angles and walked slowly towards the ruin of a building, the entrance to which was still partly there. Stepping through he peered into the blackness. Someone struck a match. The match was extinguished immediately, but it served its purpose. Huntingdon walked straight to Kocker.

They shook hands. It was an eerie sensation.

'You spoke to your people?'

'I did.' They spoke in whispers.

'You now trust me?'

'We do.'

'And I can trust you.'

'Of course.'

'Did you like the way we helped bring down the British Government?'

Huntingdon wondered what Kocker was getting at. He let him go on.

'War is the best time for revolution, my Vicar ... Perhaps ninety per cent of your fighting forces are working-class, yes? Of that you will agree ... but would it surprise you to know that perhaps twenty per cent of those have communist sympathies? Our people, among yours, have been spreading propaganda for some time. They impress among their fellow-soldiers that the ordinary working man should no longer have to depend on a living on the whims of the wealthy.

Huntingdon said nothing.

'World domination was what Lenin preached, my Vicar ...

'Quite so, Kocker, but we can't stay here and talk about politics.'

'No, you are right. I have more information for you. It concerns spying and spies. The Western world is now riddled with an untold number of Soviet spies. They all have the same task ... to get hold of the secret of the Atom bomb.'

It shook Huntingdon, but it made sense. Stalin had been furious when he learned of the Atom drop on Japan. He had been left out while Russia was still suffering monumental losses. He had vowed revenge.

'No refugees will be allowed to work in places like that.'

Kocker's head shook in the darkness. 'Emigrés will be used as couriers and contacts. The real spies will be inside.'

'Nonsense!'

'Wait, my Vicar. Wait and see, and remember two names. They have already been approached and they have agreed to share your secrets.'

'Are you certain of this?'

'It was I who brought it about.'

'And you'll give them to me?'

'In exchange for information. I need something to make me look well in the eyes of my superiors.'

'You are still in the NKVD?'

'I always will be. Once in, I cannot get out. The only way out is death.'

Huntingdon nodded. 'There is talk that Russia will be warned ... on pain of being involved in another war ... to remove her occupying troops from Austria.'

Kocker blew through his lips. 'We could not afford to fight another war. Not now that the Americans have the Atom bomb. Now the Allies are beginning to appreciate what Moscow intends to do. However, that is valuable information. It will enable us to plan further in front.'

'Your information? The names?'

'Fuchs and Nunn-May. They are the only two I know at present.'

'I will arrange for them to be watched.'

'Be careful, my Vicar. If they are discovered too quickly, Moscow will know there is a leak. Do not catch them too soon. Let them do what we want them to for a while, then cause a scandal ... but keep one step in front. Make sure the information they give us is slightly outdated. Always keep in front.'

'Thank you, Kocker.' Huntingdon was curious to see the future.

'Be wary of the future,' Kocker seemed to be reading his mind. 'Russia will turn cold towards her old Allies.'

'I'll remember.'

'I hope so, and now I must go ... Warn the French. France is ripe for a communist takeover.'

Kocker disappeared into the darkness and left Huntingdon wondering. Time would tell.

Less than a year later the French communists topped the poll in the General Election, narrowly missing taking power. In the Russian zone of Germany communists polled the least number of votes, but using Nazi tactics of brutality and intimidation they gained power. The world began to worry. Kocker's warnings had materialised.

The next contact from Kocker came in May 1950, nearly five years to the day when they first met. It arrived in the form of a telephone call from the director of MI5, in which the caller simply said there was a message for him. Could he arrange for it to be collected?

How to get the message without being identified was a problem, and it forced him to adopt complicated methods. He arranged for the message to be taken by car to a lonely road in Kent, where he would meet the messenger at a certain location. It arrived, via a senior member of MI5, and Huntingdon arranged an odd welcome. He sat in his own car and flicked his lights in the pitch darkness and waited. The messenger extinguished his own light, got out of his car, walked into Huntingdon's blazing headlights and laid the small, sealed pouch on the bonnet of Huntingdon's car. He turned and walked away without looking back. Huntingdon switched off his lights, got out of the car, took hold of the pouch, switched his lights back on and walked away, keeping the headlights between himself and the other man. He walked for some way, then ran until he reached another minor road where a second car waited and drove back to London.

The message from Kocker was explicit. The Russian said first that a Polish diplomat would be the courier. It would always be a Polish diplomat. The Vicar need not concern himself with the workings of the arrangement; just that his courier would always be a Polish diplomat.

The Poles, Huntingdon knew, had no love for the Russians.

The Polish diplomat would arrange to be at a public telephone box once every month and await a call at a pre-arranged time. Information could then be passed on, unless the Vicar wished to choose another method.

The rest of the message was riveting. It told Huntingdon that a month later the North Korean communists would invade the South Korean pro-West republic, and that a group calling itself the Viet Minh would begin a campaign to throw the French out of Indo-China by force.

Huntindon passed the information on and suggested that the American President be informed, then began the business of preparing for further messages from Kocker. Two people were recruited by telephone, a man and a woman, who in turn recruited others. He arranged for his employees to fetch and carry when the time came to exchange or receive information, and when the Korean War reaches its height information came thick and fast. It became necessary after a time for one of his staff to meet the courier, since too many visits to a telephone box would arouse suspicion. It then became standard practice for the information to be exchanged in a variety of places. It might be a tube-train in the rush hour or in a crowded store, or at a football match, and then everything was relayed to him by telephone.

Eventually he had to have a cover and he arranged for his own staff to become a branch of the cypher department of SIS. The department grew. SIS was disbanded and embraced by DI6, and the heads of the Intelligence departments died one by one, leaving behind a code-name and a telephone number for their successors. The two original members of the staff also died over the years and Balquidder was recruited. Balquidder became one of only three people who could speak to him, and no one now knew his name. The procedure was fool-proof.

In time the Reciprocal Information Pact began.

Nine

Edward Anderson, sometimes known as David Noble, was picked up some hours after Balquidder left the pub. He was sitting reading a paper in the departure lounge at West London air terminal, awaiting the arrival of the airport bus that would transport him to Heathrow. Two men joined him, one either side.

'Edward Anderson?' The man on his left asked.

'Yessir.' Anderson used an American accent.

'Do you have any kind of identification about you, Mr Anderson?'

'Yeah ...' Anderson moved his hand into his inside pocket, then stopped. What were they playing at? Of course he would have identification if he was travelling by air.

'Who are you guys?' He took his hand away.

'Police, Mr Anderson.'

'You got ID?'

The two men produced the necessary credentials, inducing Anderson to do likewise.

'Thank you, Mr Anderson.' The speaker said. 'Now, sir. Would you quietly and gently pick up your bag and come with us, please.'

'What for? What the—'

'Just come with us, sir, and please don't make any scenes. Cameras are recording every movement you make. Violent scenes from an arrested man don't do him any good in court, sir.'

'Arrested? What are you guys—'

'Yes, Mr Anderson, sir. You are under arrest and you will shortly be charged with the murder of the late Patricia Birdsall.'

Anderson froze.

'As I say, Mr Anderson,' the speaker repeated. 'Don't make any scenes.'

'Okay, okay. What's it all about? I didn't kill no broad.'

'That is not for us to decide, sir. Please come along.'

Anderson picked up his overnight bag and rose. With the two men flanking him he walked casually from the terminal building. On cue, a car emerged from the underground car-park and pulled alongside, and in a matter of seconds they were in a row on the back seat.

'You guys are making a mistake,' said Anderson. 'You'll have to release me when I make my telephone call.'

'Please shut up, sir.' One of them said, bored.

Anderson took note of where they were going. It was obvious that they weren't headed for a local police station. He shrugged. As soon as Rogal knew he had been lifted he'd be out.

They entered the heavy traffic of Central London, out the other side into Commercial Road. The driver took a left turn and Anderson found himself transported back to Victorian London. The street was narrow, with buildings of four floors on either side. The narrow confines gave the impression that the buildings were much higher, but there was no mistaking their age. They were old and decrepit; some windows and doors were boarded up and slogans of every sort had been sprayed on walls. It was a bumpy ride and through the windscreen Anderson could see the small cobbles peppering the street ahead. He knew of no police station or of any kind of safe houses in the area and it began to worry him.

To their right was an old warehouse. It looked older than the houses in the streets. All its windows, high off the ground, were boarded up, but its large double doors opened easily ... closing again when the car drove into the gloom of the empty building.

'Out you get, sir.'

Chinks of light broke through gaps in the boarded-up windows and after some seconds Anderson could make out his surroundings. The floor of the warehouse was cobbled like the street outside and the walls were dirty and covered with cobwebs. The air smelled, and the only other thing in sight apart

58

from the car was a flight of wooden steps leading to a door.

They mounted the steps, the door opening before they reached it. There was a darkened hallway on the other side of the door, no lights, and on the other side of the hallway was another door.

The second door opened automatically and Anderson was amazed at what he saw. It was a plush office, to the point of being luxurious. On the floor in front of him was his suitcase that he thought was now on its way to America. A man was in the office sitting behind a desk.

'Come in, Mr Anderson. Take a pew, old thing.'

Anderson accepted the invitation and guessed who the other man was.

'My name is Balquidder. Perhaps you've heard of me?'

Anderson nodded. He looked at Balquidder, confident. The Englishman was like an overgrown schoolboy. He could handle him.

'You've rather overstepped the mark, old thing,' sighed Balquidder, putting on an admonishing but jovial manner. 'Murder is a crime in this country, you know. Can't have that, you know.'

'Shit!' Anderson snapped back. 'I haven't harmed anyone in my life.'

The statement was true. Anderson was considered to be an expert on women. He had a silver tongue and never had to resort to violence.

'Until now, old thing. Unfortunately the drug you administered to Miss Birdsall did not agree with her. You see, Miss Birdsall suffered from a rare condition that made her body absorb certain drugs quickly, and not reject or fight them. The drug you gave her, considering her rare position, was deadly poison.'

Anderson said nothing. It was possible. He'd heard of cases like it.

'Your fingerprints are all over Miss Birdsall's flat, Mr Anderson, and on the glass that contained the poison, so we have you by the old cobblers, what?'

'I didn't know,' said Anderson. It was pointless denying it. His prints were all over the flat. Christ, he couldn't have foresaw that she was that way.

'Doesn't matter, old thing. When you come up before the beak, Miss Birdsall's condition won't be mentioned. You will be charged with murdering her by using a deadly poison, and it will come out that you work for the CIA.'

'My chief won't allow you to get that far.'

'Mr Rogal? Dear chap won't know until you actually stand trial. You'll be charged in camera, you see.'

Anderson shook his head. 'Rogal will stop you. He has influence over here.'

'Has he, indeed? I wonder, with whom?'

'You'll find out in due course.'

'Dear, dear. You're such an impetuous fellow. ...'

Balquidder rose and pointed to the window behind him. 'I want you to look at the glass in that window, old thing. This ...' Balquidder took a gun from his desk. '... is a deadly weapon. You hold the dashed thing like this, see ... And insert these stubby things into these little holes ... Jolly fun, isn't it?' Balquidder behaved as if Anderson was a child learning how to play a new game. 'One points it ...' He pointed the gun at the window. 'Squeezes this small curved lever ... And the nasty little pieces of metal that come out the other end do so at a terrible rate of knots ... Strewth, they can make a terrible mess of a person's body. That's why only grown men should handle them ... Nasty devils.'

The gun went off and the bullet smashed against the glass in the window. Anderson ducked when the bullet bounced off and plunged into the wood panelling on the wall.

'Special glass, old thing. As is the glass in the windows in the apartment next door, which will be your home for a little while until I decide what to do with you. Just a suggestion that you don't attempt to break your way out. It can't be done.'

'Hey, what are you guys up to? You can't kidnap someone.'

'We just want to keep you safe, old thing.'

'You'll never get away with it.'

'I believe you're right-handed?'

Anderson nodded.

Balquidder shot him through the left shoulder.

'That should keep you quiet for a while, old thing.'

60

Ten

Rogal had men out looking for Anderson. Anderson had to be got out of the country fast. After the conversation with Balquidder the agent's life wasn't worth a plugged nickel; had he realised that at the time he'd have had Anderson over in Washington for de-briefing immediately after the incident. He'd checked out of the apartment he'd been allocated and taken a taxi to the air terminal. Both he and his baggage had been checked in, but the trail ended there. He'd vanished.

Mellini was unhappy when he heard. Losing an agent in an unfriendly country was bad enough, but losing one in a friendly country was worse.

It taught Rogal two things. The President's warning not to underestimate the British became reality. Balquidder, and whoever controlled him, were more ruthless than the KGB. To himself he admitted that he had underestimated Balquidder, but it also taught him that the British were afraid. To lift an American agent in London, knowing that the CIA would know, indicated that they were prepared to go to any length to protect their man. That being the case, he would have to go to any length to find him.

He received a telephone call that boosted his confidence.

'Chief! There's a guy left Balquidder's office. He took a cab and asked to be taken to Heathrow, and he has a Diplomatic pouch with him.'

'Follow him. But don't let him get to the end of the line.'

'Right, chief.'

Ken Penton felt proud. He had been working for Intelligence for three years as a junior messenger and now they'd suddenly chosen him for a big one. It had been sudden, too. One minute he was behind his desk preparing project sheets to take to the next floor down, and the next he was in the superintendent's office being asked if he would like to go to Finland.

No one else was available, the superintendent told him. All senior messengers — what the public called spies — were out on projects and something important had cropped up. He had been watched during the three years with the department and they were more than satisfied with his progress. He was, the superintendent said, ready for outside work.

He'd hidden his feelings. Elated, he'd felt like jumping over the desk and kissing the old boy, but he managed to stand and behave as if he'd been told to make the tea.

There was an important message to be taken to a contact in Finland for quick despatch into the Soviet Union, and since many of the messengers were known anyway, a fresh face was ideal. No one knew him; he was capable, and the information was important. He would telephone his young wife and tell her he'd be away for two or three days. He should tell her that he was accompanying one of his superiors to Paris and there would be no time to go home first. Following a lengthy briefing a taxi took him to Old Broad Street where all the arrangements were being made.

The department had arranged a first-class flight to Helsinki and he wallowed in the luxury of the sectioned-off area at the front of the 707. The small attaché case was chained to his wrist. What was inside he had no idea. Neither could he get in to find out. His contact, Kupo Kokkonen, had the key. There were five other passengers; two elderly couples and a blonde girl. The blonde, he mused, would be a Finn. He smiled thinly at them all, acknowledging their presence aboard, then lay back to await take-off.

Two latecomers rushed aboard at the last minute puffing and panting and apologised for holding the others up. Penton smiled and waved his hand for them to slow down; his watch said they were not due to leave for several minutes. The couple were English by the sound of them, fortyish and not unused to flying. They took the seat across the aisle and strapped themselves in without looking.

It was a lonely flight. The two elderly couples dozed off and the couple who'd arrived late didn't stop talking to each other. The girl – he tried often to catch her eye – never lifted her head out of soppy magazines. Only the two stewardesses kept him from being completely alone.

The two elderly couples left the plane during the stop-over in Copenhagen, and a number of people got on. Two of them were girls, blondes like the first girl. Each of them gave a little smile. But still no one spoke to him.

It took four hours to reach Helsinki and there at least someone did speak to him. He was met by one of the department's people 'in-situ'; she was perhaps ten years his elder. Varla, she called herself. Fussing over him as if he were a child embarrassed him, but he welcomed being installed in a luxury hotel overlooking the harbour.

Varla was to stay with him until he continued his journey. She had their meals brought to the suite and afterwards, like a fussing mother, she did the clearing up. She even put him to bed, still with the attaché case chained to his wrist, and sat in a chair nearby while he slept.

Next morning they said their farewells at Helsinki's main railway station. Penton's train was due to depart at 10.

Two platforms away the man watching them from inside a telephone kiosk spoke rapidly into the receiver:

'Tell the chief that he stayed the night with Varla Torne. She met him at the airport and is seeing him off.'

Rogal received the message within the hour. Varla Torne was one of the most important British agents in Northern Scandinavia. She ran a group that constantly ferried information from over the border. No one had been able to discover her methods. She was good, and if she was being used it meant that something big was on. The trail would lead to Prairie Dog.

Penton enjoyed the train journey. It was a long trip, but the scenery was beautiful and most people sharing his compartment seemed only too pleased to speak to him. They queried the attaché case chained to his wrist and he offered the statutory reply. He was a businessman hoping to complete a contract and until the contract was signed he couldn't afford to let it out of his sight. His fellow passengers nodded. Industrial espionage was a terrible thing.

It took twelve hours to travel the 350 miles to Lieksa, and it was pitch dark when he arrived. There were few street lamps, most of the lighting available coming from houses and shops. It surprised him that the shops were still open, but it was refreshing to see people about at that time of night. Snow was falling and it was bitter cold. He was glad when he reached the small hotel Varla had booked him in at.

Penton slept well. The journey had tired him out as Varla had warned him it would. When he woke in the morning the ground outside was covered thickly with snow. Lieska was a picture of beauty with the snow covering the log-built houses and it reminded him of a Christmas card. Then he saw the card that had been pushed under the door. Kokkonen would contact him, he had been told, and he was to follow the instructions to the letter.

The message on the card told him not to have breakfast, to leave by the side entrance and walk towards the taxi rank. He would be collected.

Penton checked the chain round his wrist, pulled his overcoat closer to his body and left the room. One short flight of stairs took him to the ground floor. A radio was playing somewhere and the smell of cooking caught his nostrils. No one seemed to be about and the side door was open. Outside someone had swept away the snow and deliverymen had left packages. Salt had been laid on the road sometime earlier and he stepped out to get away from the deep drifts against the buildings. It was still dark. He was very far north and it would be afternoon before the few hours of daylight came.

Some hundred yards along the road was the taxi rank. It had a sign illuminated by a dim light above it. Below the sign was a dark-coloured car with its windows steamed over. A rear door opened as he approached and he climbed in, catching his breath in the thick tobacco smoke.

'Good morning, Mr Penton.'

Penton moved his head and saw the woman who'd arrived on the plane late. The man was driving, and the woman had a

64

gun pointed at his mouth.

'Good Lord!' He gasped. Something had gone wrong.

'Please undo the chain, Mr Penton.' The woman said.

'I ... I ... but you're not ...'

'Correct. We're not the people you're supposed to meet.'

The car began to move and fear built up in Penton. No one had said anything about guns.

Eleven

Balquidder looked smart when the Bentley picked him up in Old Broad Street. His new clothes showed him to be a man of means and his brolly and bowler indicated that he was a man of authority. But it was the attaché case in his right hand that interested the men watching him.

The Bentley pulled into the traffic and a taxi followed, keeping three cars behind and radioing their progress to Rogal. Balquidder knew they would be there, but it didn't worry him. He sank into the deep upholstery and read through the *Financial Times*.

They followed him to the airport and noted his destination, then bought tickets on the same flight to Paris. They sat four rows behind during the short flight, fidgeting while he relaxed, and when the plane halted opposite the terminal building at Charles de Gaulle airport they let him get off first. Two other men took over, having to hurry to get through the crowds thronging the customs hall. Balquidder detoured. His diplomatic pass took him past customs and immigration alike, through a special exit designed for that purpose, getting him to the taxi rank long before his followers.

He waited for them to catch up, never having looked back once, and waved to the driver of a black Mercedes. The two men skidded to a halt when they saw him still not departed and waved for their own car to come alongside them. They became excited, too; for the driver of the Mercedes was Chinese.

One of the men stayed behind to call Rogal in London, the other following Balquidder. The Mercedes didn't hurry but weaved its way gently through the heavy traffic, taking double the amount of time normally spent driving into the city. It finally halted outside Maxim's restaurant where Balquidder alighted. From Maxim's a second Oriental appeared and smiled warmly at him. The two shook hands and went inside.

Roger Bonet gulped. He had been ordered to watch Balquidder like a hawk. On no account had he to lose him. He jumped out of his car, abandoning it by the side of the road, and hurried into the restaurant. Balquidder was there, removing his coat and laughing with the Oriental. Bonet watched amazed. He could imagine Rogal's reaction. What in hell did someone from British Intelligence want with the Chinese Mission in Paris?

Bonet was even more amazed when he saw the Oriental Balquidder had come to meet. Sitting alone in an alcove was Chai Li Huan. Huan, Bonet knew, was directly responsible for China's massive spending spree in the West. China was investing billions of dollars to modernise her industry and all the major Western nations were competing for the contracts. And Huan also ran Peking's massive spy network, a web that stretched around the world.

Balquidder's escort left him at the alcove and retired to a nearby table. Huan rose and shook Balquidder's hands, both hands, and kissed each other's cheeks continental fashion. Lunch was ordered, and when the first course arrived they began talking. Bonet swore. He had been taught to lip-read, but the shape of the alcove prevented his seeing their mouths. Only their eyes and the top of their heads were visible. He called for a telephone and kept watch.

'Well, Mr Balquidder,' said Huan. 'To say that I was surprised to learn of your visit to Paris would be an understatement. However, it is pleasant to meet you.'

'Thank you, Mr Huan.' Balquidder put on a perfect show of diplomacy. 'And I would like to remark that it is an honour for me to meet the venerated Chai Li Huan.'

Huan bowed slightly. 'Your words are kind, Mr Balquidder, and I accept them in the spirit they were offered.'

'Truth is always difficult to express, Mr Huan. In this world today there is so much that causes anger and resentment, and personalities are used by some to create bad impressions. That is why I deem it an honour to be in the company of one who, regardless of his belief in the spectrum of social structure, is highly respected in diplomatic circles.'

Balquidder lifted his spoon to his mouth. There was a procedure which had to be followed before the subject of business began. The Chinese liked to be treated as equal of Westerners and not as second-hand Orientals.

'It is a pleasure to speak with you, Mr Balquidder. One only wishes that other civilised nations possessed English manners and their art of diplomacy.'

'And likewise, sir. It is equally a pleasure to speak with a gentleman who dislikes the brash modern methods of conducting business.'

'Ye-es, our business. …'

Balquidder had to be careful. One or the other had eventually to bring the subject to life, but it had to be done in such a way that it would appear to evolve from their conversation. It was a complete farce, but it was the way it was done. To all intents and purposes they were just two men coming across each other and finding they had many things in common.

'A very bright consomme, this,' commented Balquidder.

'Yes, I must admit that I look forward to lunch in Maxims … Were you chosen especially to meet me?'

'Yes. Someone decided that I was better suited for this kind of meeting. I must say I was rather flattered.'

'You have the Oriental flair for modesty, Mr Balquidder. Most gracious, I would say … Rather an unusual meeting?'

'Quite … Maxims does a lovely paté … My government wonders if you would consider rearranging your contracts in the West.'

'I quite like the way they braise onions … I understand we had completed our industrial contracts.'

'I see … Shall we have the next course?'

They went through the next course in silence. Balquidder wanted Huan to have time to think about why the suggestion was being put forward. A firm reply would come later.

Huan had only recently placed a $2-billion contract with a major corporation in California, to supply China over a period of ten years with sufficient electronic equipment to bring her up to date with the rest of the world.

'Could your larger companies compete? … We must have

68

more wine.'

'Given the contract they could surpass anything our American colleagues can achieve ... I'll order the wine.'

'Please ... And what do you offer in return?'

'A highly-placed Washington spy in the Kremlin.' Balquidder said softly, without looking up.

Huan nodded, but not committing himself. 'You know his name? ... The onion is underdone.'

'I'll call someone and have a fresh course brought immediately ... No, unfortunately we don't know his name ... Ah! The waiter's spotted us ... We only know that he is one of four people.'

'Mmm, interesting ... Unusual for Maxims to fall on something.'

'The 2nd Directorate of External Planning ... Yes, shame rather ... One of the four section heads.'

'I agree ... However, the excellent game made up, I think, for the failure of the onion ... I will have the alteration in the contract tenders taken in hand immediately. You will hear from us.'

'An excellent meal, Mr Huan. One can never diverse from the fact that the French are remarkable chefs.'

'Quite so, Mr Balquidder. You will allow me to nave you as my guest?'

'Most certainly, Mr Huan. I could never refuse the offer of a gentleman.'

'Thank you, Mr Balquidder,' Huan beamed, his stained teeth showing and revolting Balquidder.

They talked nonsense until the meal was finished, the subject matter of their business now closed and forgotten for the time being.

'A most satisfying and enjoyable lunch, Mr Huan. You have my sincere gratitude and undying respect.' Balquidder rose.

Huan lumbered to his feet. He was twice as old as Balquidder.

'It was my pleasure to have lunched with you, Mr Balquidder.'

'I hope I have the honour again, Mr Huan.'

Huan smiled, bowed in respect and sat down. Balquidder

smiled, handed his attaché case to the escort and marched proudly from Maxims. Huan only had to take the necessary papers from the case, sign them and return them to London along with the Peking contracts.

Bonet got up from his table and followed Balquidder to the airport, a question mark hanging over what they had talked about. Balquidder was back in London in time for dinner.

The Vicar was pleased. He had chosen well in Balquidder. Not only had they given Washington's top spy to Peking, ruining America's infiltration of the Kremlin; they had also gained for Britain a lucrative contract. America had lost twice over. And with a bit of luck the Chinese gentlemen would make a complete balls-up when he went after the American spy.

The name of the American spy in the Kremlin was well known to Balquidder and the Vicar, but giving it to Huan would be too much of a giveaway. Huan would have known there was something behind the move, but giving him just enough to whet his appetite would arouse no suspicions. And just enough was all Huan would require. It would brook no difficulties in finding a spy among four men. It would help to take some of the heat off Kocker. But not all.

Ken Penton was terrified. The ugly snout of the silenced gun was something he'd never seen before, except in films, and the woman holding it looked as if she knew what she was doing. The couple said nothing as the car left Lieska behind, and although they passed cars going in the opposite direction Penton was too scared to try to attract attention.

Lieska soon disappeared and there was nothing but snow and dense forest. The forests stretched for miles alongside the lonely road and every so often a narrow road or lane cut off at right angles. The car turned into one of the narrow roads and continued for a mile, then stopped. The woman moved the gun and Penton relaxed, but only for a split second. The snout of the silencer moved down and the gun jerked slightly against the woman's hand. A bullet smashed into Penton's wrist, severing through the light chain attached to the case and driving the remnants of the broken links into his wrist and arm.

Penton looked down at his wrist for a second, his eyes and mouth wide, then up at the woman, and then screamed as the realisation of what had happened reached his brain. The woman ignored him and snatched away the attaché case. It wouldn't open and she demanded the key.

'There is none!' Penton gasped.

The woman shot him again, this time in the crotch, the shock bringing a noise like a high-pitched wheeze from Penton's throat. Another shot disposed of the lock and the case fell open. From it the woman took a small parcel. Unwrapped it revealed a leaflet.

It was an ordinary leaflet, printed in English, but publicising a rummage sale auspiced by a branch of the communist party.

BARGAINS!!
NOTTINGHAM PEOPLES' EXECUTIVE.
RUMMAGE SALE AND FÊTE.
SATURDAY 17TH FEBRUARY 1968.
DAWSON HALL, ASH STREET.
1.30 PM.

'What does this mean?' The woman demanded.

Penton could only shake his head. The woman took the movement of his head as a sign of defiance. Apart from the initial scream when she'd shot his wrist he'd only gasped and wheezed. He hadn't screamed again, or even moaned. The woman and her companion took this as a sign that he was an experienced agent. Men with high-intensity training rarely gave way. But it was simply that Penton's numbed brain did not know what to do. The woman looked up at him. There was no fear in his face now, only blatant disbelief.

Penton hoped he was dreaming. From the waist down he was drenched in blood; and the fabric upholstery of the seat was looking like a sponge. The woman shot him through the head.

Twelve

The 2nd Directorate of External Planning is directly responsible to the Supreme Soviet for its actions. It is split into four sections, each with a section head responsible to a Director. The four section heads have restricted access to information, knowing only whatever information passes through his administration, but each director has access to all information from the sections, and this he reports in person to the Supreme Soviet.

The Directorate arranges and organises the transportation of information from Soviet spies around the world to the nerve centre in the Kremlin, and not until the information reaches the conference table of the Supreme Soviet is it studied and acted on.

The 1st Directorate of External Planning performs the opposite task. All signals and messages sent out to Soviet spies around the world are channelled solely through its administration. This method of communication and transportation is used as a precaution against Kremlin employees being able to compare questions with answers. And it is a successful method. A foreign spy cannot make use of a reply unless he first knows the question, and vice-versa.

There are two other Directorates: the 1st and 2nd Directorates of Internal Planning, carrying out the same tasks but on a domestic scale. All four Directorates are constructed exactly the same, and, as in every security organisation in the world, it has a flaw.

The Kremlin's methods of making access to classified information impossible or extremely difficult is unique. It has developed further on the ancient adage of the right hand not knowing what the left hand is doing. Its construction and accessibility makes it impossible for one finger on one hand to know what the other fingers are doing.

The flaw lies in the fact that all four Directors make their reports together, when the information is compared and studied, and when the hands recognise each other. Each day at 0850 Moscow time the Supreme Soviet meets, going over the minutes of the previous day's meeting, then listening from 0900 to 1000 to the reports of the four Directors. During this hour the Soviet Union is at its most vulnerable.

News of the presence of an Allied spy highly placed in the Kremlin did not come through the normal Directorate channels but directly by diplomatic courier, and it sent a wave of fear through the twenty-member Supreme Soviet. At the morning meeting following the arrival of the news, nothing was mentioned about a spy, but each of the Directors was stared at and studied by the members of the Soviet, and by the six experts from counter-Intelligence co-opted to the Soviet for the occasion. It did not matter that the Directors were high-ranking officers of the KGB.

The Directors knew instantly they saw the spy-finders that something was wrong. It put them off-balance when they made their reports, each of them sweating heavily during the hour-long ordeal. If there was a traitor in their department, they too were guilty.

'How high can he be?' the Chairman of the Supreme Soviet wanted to know.

'It is early to say, Comrade,' said Viktor Protiv, Minister of Defence.

Georgi Markova, Minister of the Interior, spoke up. 'As the report from London suggests, Comrade Chairman, our man there will learn more from the American, Rogal.'

'It is not good enough. Until then we still have a traitor in our midst.'

'We have to be extremely careful, Comrade,' Major Zibor Grest of the KGB's counter-Intelligence department said. 'If word leaks out that we know, he will go to ground, and it could take years to learn his identity. We must allow him to continue, but keeping continual watch, and when the information comes from London we can act.'

'It still isn't good enough. There must be an immediate investigation. Every section must be thoroughly investigated without delay. It must be determined who all has had any contact with anyone from the West ... Anyone! ... Employ any and every means to discover his identity.'

'What in hell did he meet the Chinaman for?' Rogal fumed. 'He must have known he would be followed.'

'Our guy over there couldn't get into a position to lip-read, chief,' one of his men said. 'But papers of some kind changed hands.'

'Yeah, but to a guy like Chai Li Huan! What the hell for? What the God-damn hell does a guy like Balquidder want with a Chinese commie? Shit! It doesn't make sense.'

'It may not have anything to do with Prairie Dog, chief.'

'Shit! ... Everything Balquidder does from now on has to do with Prairie Dog. I don't trust that sonofabitch.'

The leaflet from Finland came in soon after and Rogal called in a cypher expert to give a preliminary opinion.

'Hell ...' Rogal complained to the cypher expert. 'Chinese commies in Paris and commie leaflets from Finland! What the hell is the guy playing at?'

'It could be in the wording, chief.' The expert told him. 'Or maybe just in the capital letters. It's an unusual way of presenting something ... you notice how every letter is a capital? And the larger capitals stand out and meet you?'

'Yeah.'

'Then again that may mean nothing. It might be that just looking at this will be sufficient. To receive this might be a kind of warning.'

'But, hell, it's twelve years old.'

The expert shrugged his shoulders. 'Could've been specifically kept for the purpose of a red warning.'

'Right. Get a team on it right away. I want to know what it says, and I don't want it today or tomorrow ... I want it yesterday!'

Rogal sent a report to Washington. Progress was slow, but the British were in a panic. They'd sent a guy not known to the

74

Agency over to Finland with a coded message for Prairie Dog. The Agency had intercepted it and was now in the process of having it de-coded. All Balquidder's people were under observation and a fly couldn't find its way through the screen. When contact was made with Prairie Dog, they would be waiting.

Rogal hoped he could live up to the contents of the report. Anderson was missing and hadn't checked in, and the woman was dead. Anderson wouldn't have killed her. Anderson couldn't kill anyone; he was a ladies man.

He was worried, though. He's turned up nothing but the leaflet, and unless it could be de-cyphered they were in trouble. All the same, he thought, it hadn't reached Prairie Dog; which meant that they'd try again. He would have to be ready to pounce.

It was time for lunch, Rogal decided. He called the restaurant in the West End, using the name Jennings to book his table. He went through the usual procedure of going by tube to Waterloo Station and making contact, then after wasting some time took a taxi to the West End.

After a half-hour and Petrokovic still hadn't appeared he began to worry for the Russian. Petrokovic would simply disappear if he were found out. Spies in the Soviet Union sometimes did not stand trial as they did in the West, particularly if they were Russian nationals and held important positions; they were generally tortured into telling all they knew and then murdered. When an hour had gone by Rogal got up and left.

Back at the embassy he sent for the couple who had taken Penton. Word was passed on, but the couple had vanished.

Major Zibor Grest began the investigation. It would be a massive undertaking, he accepted. Every single person working in all the Directorates was under suspicion, most of all the four Directors; hundreds of men and women who years before had been vetted by the KGB. Nothing had been overlooked when their backgrounds were examined, every single minute of their lives since they'd first attended school being carefully plotted.

He began with the Directors. Their judgement was seldom

ignored when information from the West came through. Their being involved in treasonable acts seemed unbelievable, yet, for some reason not yet explained, in the past it had always been people of their calibre who had turned traitor.

Leonev Chukotev, head of the 2nd Directorate of External Planning, was one of the old school. With many others he had fought across two thousand miles of Europe during Russia's sacrifice to defeat the Nazi invader. It had won him medals, and two years in prison when Stalin decided to punish those who had seen the West. He had made many western contacts, which alone could have condemned him to death, but after two years in Siberia he was recalled to develop the contacts into spying against their own countries.

Chukotev's gift was that he did not need the services of a computer. Every signal that had ever passed through his hands was now permanently stored in his brain. In a matter of seconds he could recall to memory anything he had filed mentally away. He was sixty-seven, looking much older, but such was his value to the KGB that they could not afford to let him retire.

Mikell Orlov, head of the 1st Directorate, had seen much more of the West than any of the others. But that was in the past. He was only fifty-nine, but gone were the days when he dined and danced in foreign embassies in different parts of the world. They had been good days, he recalled. There had been no pressures on him during the day, and the evenings had been his own. But there had been an indiscretion with a French diplomat's wife, a complaint was made, and they'd recalled him. The episode scared him and he expected exile in the East; instead they put him into the Directorate as a punishment. There he would have to behave himself. It was like a prison. But he'd worked hard and been promoted several times.

Jeka Mitkin, the head of the 2nd Directorate of Internal Planning was something different, part of which was being a homosexual. He was in his mid-sixties but insisted on wearing American jeans to work. Small and fat, he was a disgusting creature when wearing his jeans, but his own ego didn't see himself that way. He was suspect, but he couldn't be demoted. He knew more than anyone how to break a code, and it was his key to success, the key to the Western clothing he bought at the 'special stores'; to the succession of young students from African nations and Russia's own constituent republics.

Running the 1st Directorate of Internal Planning was Lev Talanov. Talanov, sixty, was a Hero of the Soviet Union. He had won them all: the Order of Lenin, the Order of the Red Banner, and a host of other coveted awards. At the battle of Kursk in the Ukraine, when 3,000 tanks pitted themselves against each other in the biggest land battle of the Second World War, he had knocked out twenty-seven enemy tanks while his own machine was immobilised with its tracks blown off.

By the time Talanov reached thirty he looked twenty years older. The war aged him prematurely and sympathy played a large part when promotions were due. No one forgot the saga of Lev Talanov and when he reached his fortieth birthday he was given his present position. But now he was fragile and hard of hearing, and so far as the KGB knew he had never been in contact with anyone from the West.

Grest admired Talanov, as he did the others for the work they performed for the Russian people, but none of them were untouchable. Grest chose Talanov's department to investigate first, his presence spreading a wave of fear through the numerous offices.

Grest was a handsome figure. He was more Nordic-looking than Russian. He stood exactly 6 ft and had blonde hair swept to one side. His blue eyes were piercing when angry, but caring when he was pleased. He still had his own teeth, forever sparkling, melting the hearts of his many lady companions when he smiled. His manner was charming, always polite and quiet, and in the company of Western diplomats could converse intimately on the subject of food and drink. He could be the perfect host, or the perfect guest, but just his presence in Talanov's department was sufficient to make everyone afraid. Everyone knew why he was there, but who was he after ...?

In the midst of the terror that gripped the Supreme Soviet, Kocker watched events pass, and when times of importance reached his ears he took the necessary steps.

The news that the US had lost the giant Chinese contract came as a bombshell to the White House. One large corporation had already spent a million dollars preparing for the contracts that would have earned them a billion, and suddenly it was cancelled. No reason was given other that it had been decided in Peking that Britain was in a better position to supply China's needs. Rogal knew instantly that Balquidder had had something to do with it. He demanded a meeting as soon as possible.

Balquidder knew what was coming but didn't jump to defend himself. Behaving in the manner of a busy man, he asked Rogal to contact his secretary to find a date and a time when he was free. They met over lunch at Balquidder's club three days later. Rogal was seething.

'Serve a dashed good meal here, Ray.' Balquidder portrayed the perfect gentleman. 'I'm certain you'll like it.'

'I couldn't give a God-damned shit about the grub!' Rogal hissed. 'I want answers to some questions.'

'Fire away, old chap.' Balquidder waved his appreciation to the waiter.

'What the hell are you playing at, Balquidder?'

'Playing at, old chap?'

'Jesus! ... Listen, fella. I want to know why you fucked up out "chip" contract with the chinks; and why you've lifted three of my people?'

'Can't help you, I'm afraid ... Don't know what you're going on about.'

Rogal hadn't touched his food. 'You want me to spell it out for you, your trip to Maxim's in Paris?'

'Maxim's?' Balquidder put his elbows on the table, his chin on his knuckles, eyes half-closed. '... Ah! Some fond memories I have of that fine tea-room.'

'You were there. I had you followed.'

'... Yes, some fond memories ... You were saying?'

Rogal's face was twisting with anger. 'You trying to start a war, or something?'

'War? Good gracious, no! We don't start wars, Ray, old chap. We just fight them ... and win them.'

'Okay, where's my three people?'

'People?' Balquidder was irritating Rogal.

'Yeah. Anderson and the Brands.'

'I sincerely hope all three have left the country by now. The two people they disposed of have many friends, friends who are extremely angry.'

'Come off it, Balquidder. I want to know what you've done with them.'

'Jolly fine piece of ...'

Rogal suddenly stood up, fuming. 'You make me sick!' He turned to leave.

'Sit down, sit down.' Balquidder said casually. 'There is something I think you should know ...'

Rogal sat down again.

'Give!'

'My trip to Paris.' Balquidder remained casual. 'I discovered something, you see, and I had to put it to the test. Thought I would help you out, old chap.'

'What the hell ...'

'There is a man they call Capuchin ...'

Rogal gasped. Capuchin was Washington's man in the Kremlin. London did know. Balquidder didn't look at Rogal. He looked down at the feast in front of him and when the fork went up to his mouth his eyes wandered around the dining-room.

'I learned ... simply out of the blue, that this man Capuchin is working for a certain Western power, and ...' He took another mouthful of food.

'Yeah?'

Balquidder had Rogal hooked. The deliberate antagonism had its effect. It was time now to spring the surprise. Mentioning Capuchin had taken some of the wind out of the American's sails. He would soon be calmed.

'... that he also works for the Chinese.'

Rogal's mouth fell open. He didnt want to believe it, but he had to hear more.

'What are you trying to sell me?'

'Just this, old chap.' Balquidder raised his eyes and looked into Rogal's, imploring. 'What was it better to lose? Capuchin or the contract?'

'What do you mean?' Rogal was bitten.

'We knew Capuchin was your man, but we didn't know about his connection with Peking. I had a chat with Mr Huan when I heard the gossip and offered him a deal. I suggested that if he didn't transfer the contract, I would inform my American colleagues that Capuchin was working for two employers. Mr Huan believes that I will never mention the fact to you, now that he has given our chaps the contract. However, while doing ourselves a favour, there is no harm in doing you a favour. I thought you would like to know.'

'You serious?' Rogal was eager.

'Never was more serious in my life.' Balquidder deliberately left off the "old chap".

'Nah!' Rogal changed suddenly. 'I can't take that.' It was too fantastic now that he'd had a second or two to think about it.

'Well, I've told you. But, remember, if I hadn't offered Mr Huan a deal, told him that I was telling you ... what would have happened to Capuchin?'

Capuchin would have been bumped off by Peking. But that didn't mean to say Balquidder was telling the truth.

'Okay, if you're going out of your way to help us, why did you lift Anderson and the Brands?'

'I didn't, old chap.'

'Then, who the hell—?'

'Peking, perhaps?'

'For what, for Christ sake?'

'To turn them into doublers?'

Balquidder paused. That was highly possible.

'Anything can happen, I suppose.' Balquidder threw in.

The Englishman was convincing. The Chinese angle was something they hadn't thought of. And it was one of the things a security service dreaded.

Rogal nodded. 'Okay, for the time being I'll take you word for it. You're obviously better placed than us to get that kind of information ... I'm sorry about the guy in Finland.'

'Don't know what you're talking about, old chap.'

'A guy called Penton.'

Balquidder shook his head. 'Just one thing I thought I might ask you to be careful about, old chap. I should watch where you're treading. If people like us make too much noise, a few Ivans will wonder why and begin asking questions themselves. Do you get my meaning?'

Rogal nodded.

'Perhaps we'll have lunch another day?'

'Yeah, perhaps ...'

Rogal went to a telephone, rang an unlisted number and snarled into the mouthpiece. 'Get word to Jesuit! Ask him to find out if Capuchin is working for the Chinks! ... And what about the God-damned leaflet?'

Rogal wouldn't settle until he was sure about Capuchin.

Thirteen

Major Zibor Grest knew his job. If there was a traitor in their midst he would find him. It would take time, but in the end he would find him. Of that he was certain.

Over the course of some days he read through the files on the four directors a number of times. He was not necessarily looking for something that would implicate any one of them, but he knew that there would be something that would implicate someone.

Each time he read he found nothing, but it did not deter him. He went on to the files of the section heads of each Directorate, then studied the reports made by each person for comparison.

He studied the signals brought in, comparing them with the reports, and arrived at the meeting of Rogal and Balquidder. He stopped then, referring to the thick files on each man, and studied in more detail.

Rogal he knew most about. In fact there was little the KGB did not know about the American; some they had learned to their benefit and some to their cost. Rogal was useful to his employer but, Grest reasoned, he lacked the subtlety of the English.

What the two men had talked about would remain a mystery. He'd had the basic theme from Petrokovic, but the exact words would never be known. Had they been minor employees in their organisations he could have them lifted and put through interrogation, but they were at a level where they became untouchable. There were some rules that even the KGB played to.

Petrokovic had stated that the two men had argued over information contained in RIP, and Petrokovic was completely reliable. The Americans were unhappy because they were not receiving their fair share of information, and things had happened since.

Rogal's boss was Mellini, but it had never been established if, in fact, Balquidder had a boss. The Englishman always seemed to have worked independently of everyone else, yet he was a man who could easily be approached; he could be invited to lunches and dinners – any kind of function, and nine times out of ten would be there. Everyone knew him to be the head of a department in British Security, and he never disguised the fact. This was unusual since people at his level were not normally in the public eye. Balquidder had power, more power than Military Intelligence or Defence Intelligence, and that kind of power wasn't given out lightly.

Since the two men had met some incidents had occurred. One of Balquidder's employees had been having an affair with an American agent; the woman had since died and the American agent had disappeared. Another of Balquidder's people had been abducted by American agents – right in the heart of London – tortured for information and then disposed of. A third, a newcomer to the business, had been followed to Finland and disposed of. He had been carrying something to hand over to a contact in Lieksa, and the couple who had carried out the disposal had also disappeared.

Then Balquidder had gone to Paris and met with the Chinese agent Huan. Rogal's agents had become excited, and shortly after the Peking-Washington industrial deal was cancelled. Rogal and Balquidder had met again, and after some heated arguing – mostly from the American – they had seemed to come to some kind of agreement. They had calmed – or the American had – and things seemed quiet; but on leaving the meeting Rogal had gone to a telephone and shouted into it. At that stage he was either angry or afraid.

Angry at not receiving the agreed amount of information? Yes, Grest nodded to himself ... But afraid? Afraid of what? What had Balquidder said that had calmed him, but at the same time could have put fear into him? The affair was odd, confusing; but there had to be something that stood out.

Grest went over the incidents carefully, breaking them up

83

into sections and inserting his own opinion. The woman who had worked for Balquidder had been an employee of long standing. She would have access to certain information, she probably read hundreds of signals every day, but since her department was where the RIP sheets came from she would not know any more than the Americans. But the woman died after an evening out with Anderson the American agent, and the American had left her flat in a hurry, flustered. Balquidder arrived soon after. Not long after that a body was removed.

The incident was familiar to Grest. The KGB also wormed its way into people's confidences and then in one fell swoop extracted information. Everyone did it at some time or another. But what could the woman know that Rogal did not? Or did Rogal think that the woman knew something? What? She would not know who the information came from … But if Balquidder was out of the country and information arrived unexpectedly, someone would have to give it to her for computing … Therefore, if there was a traitor … It came galloping towards him … Balquidder couldn't be his controller. And if that were so then Balquidder had to have a boss.

This would be what the American was after. If Rogal was angry, then he would want to know who received the information before Balquidder's department. Someone higher up would control the traitor, but the Americans must have presumed that the woman knew who it was. She wouldn't, of course. The English did not leave that kind of information lying about. If, however, Balquidder lifted the American … Why? He would have learned nothing. That would have to be checked through.

He went on to the Finnish episode. Varla Torne was well known to the KGB. She ran an efficient group along the Finnish-Russo border. She was a thorn in their side, but again she was the type they could not dispose of. Finland was as kind to them as it was unkind. True, many traitors were spirited across the frontier by Varla Torne and taken to England and America; but so too did the frontier hide KGB spies who crossed over to Finland and could become one of a dozen nationalities. That way they escaped being photographed at West European airports.

It must have been important for Torne to take personal charge of the affair. Normally she would have sent someone to the airport to meet the agent, but she had taken the onus on herself. And the Americans had followed the newcomer. They had followed him all the way from London, as if they had been expecting a movement. They knew he was from Balquidder — or they were presuming he was — and got to him before the contact.

So what had he been carrying? What was so important to Rogal and the CIA? If Rogal was looking for the name of a controller, he would not have got it from the agent in Finland. The hidden spy — Russia's traitor — would know his controller, and would not have to be told. A message of some kind was being passed on, but what kind? To tell the traitor that something was wrong in his employer's camp? Hardly. That didn't make sense.

And there was the agent abducted in the heart of London. His knowledge of the organisation would be limited. It would simply be his job to collect and distribute information ... But he would have contacts; contacts that the Americans would not know about. Who? A contact in London? ... Like the woman? Back to a controller again? A controller the Americans want to know about?

It could well be, thought Grest, but Intelligence organisations did not entirely depend on information given to them by others. They had their own methods of obtaining information, and it was checked and double-checked before it was accepted.

Washington would double-check any information given to her by London, and vice-versa ... So if Washington, through Rogal, was angry because she wasn't receiving her fair share, and Rogal was attempting to discover a controller in London, it had to mean that both Washington and London had spies in the Kremlin. And it would mean that London's spy was higher placed than Washington's.

That was why the Americans were so upset. No wonder Rogal showed fear!

Grest delved deeper and deeper, then in the middle of a file he stopped. Rogal could not have shown fear because Balquidder had told him about a higher placed English spy. Balquidder would never have told him that. It was the sort of thing Balquidder would never have breathed a word about. But Rogal obviously knew. If he could discover the controller he could find a way to the spy – the traitor – something he must have discovered by accident. But that still didn't explain why he had shown fear. What had made him afraid? Something Balquidder had said, obviously.

The only way to find out was to ask Balquidder.

Fourteen

Nikolai Malin was eating when contact was made. He enjoyed eating out in Rotterdam. The city was cosmopolitan and the range of eating houses never seemed to end. Malin used the same restaurant each time he visited the city. They knew him there and they knew he was a Russian diplomat of some kind, but they never pressed him. He was a valued customer, always leaving a large gratuity to be shared among the staff.

He felt somewhat affronted when the head waiter asked if he would mind someone sharing his table, but tried not to appear too annoyed.

'By all means,' he said in perfect Dutch. 'I shall soon be finished.'

The stranger sat facing him, smiling apologies, and ordered lunch.

'Sorry to disturb you, but the house seems rather full today.'

'Quite all right.' Malin returned the smile and continued his meal.

He quickly studied the stranger. He was elderly, white-haired, probably a survivor from the ruins of Rotterdam. His suit was a little rumpled and his tie askew. A worried businessman.

The stranger studied Malin in turn. Malin was young, perhaps thirty, impeccably dressed – as was the style of the KGB now – not very tall but obviously powerful. It could be seen across his shoulders and chest. He boasted a Western-style haircut, the old 'Perry Como'.

Malin did not look up after their brief introduction, but between mouthfuls read through a morning newspaper. Suddenly the stranger spoke, in a low and barely audible voice.

'There is an article in the paper about Jesuits.'

The stranger saw Malin stiffen, briefly for the merest instant, then continued to eat and read.

A few minutes went by before Malin replied. It was just one word.

'Why?' He spoke into his dessert.

'Priority one.'

'I am not supposed to be contacted in person. You should know that.'

'Orders, I'm afraid.'

'What's wrong?'

'You have to determine if Capuchin could be working for Peking.'

Malin nearly dropped his spoon and a spasm went through his body. He recovered, still not looking up.

'What are you saying?'

'That is the message. You must not approach him on the subject. Just watch.'

Malin did not reply. He continued his lunch, slower than before, then paid his bill and left. The stranger moved his discarded newspaper across the table and began reading it.

Outside Malin gasped. His heart was thumping and he wanted to rush across the street, to run as fast as he could. He spotted a bar and entered, buying a beer and retiring to a corner where he could think.

Capuchin working for Peking! A shudder went through him. That would be the end of him. If it was true then Peking would know about him. The results could be disastrous all round.

He tried not to panic. In three hours he was due to return to Moscow with a diplomatic bag and he could appear unsettled. They would know straight away that something was wrong, and someone in his position would be immediately investigated.

After a second beer he returned to the Trade Mission and reported. His boss was waiting.

'You've lunched, Nikolia?'

'Yes, comrade.'

'Good. Everything is ready. You may leave when you are.'

'I'll order a car now, comrade.'

'Have a good trip, Nikolai.'

'Thanks.'

Malin went downstairs to the despatch office and signed in ... Have a good trip. That was good!

The brown attaché case was taken from the safe and handed to him. He signed for it, six forms in all, and so did the two KGB agents on either side of him. How could he, he thought, have a good trip flanked all the time by two killers?

All three left the trade mission together. Even in the car they sat either side of him and at the airport never left his side. Not with a wealth of secrets in the brown case.

He was the ideal courier, he knew. As a KGB courier he had privileges. He was trusted. He never knew what he carried — not that he could find out with the bloodhounds with him — but that was all part of his cover. As a courier he made regular trips to the West, and as a CIA courier he never carried anything except in his head. That way he could never be connected. It was all done by word of mouth. Capuchin gave him the information and it was no problem to pass it on in Rotterdam.

It had been all right until now. The CIA gave him enough money without arousing anyone's suspicions. He never pushed himself on anyone; never drew attention to himself and never asked questions. He just did as he was told. But now it was different. If Capuchin was working for two bosses his chances of survival were cut in half. There now would be a chance that the KGB's investigators would become interested in him.

But what could he do? Confess? They would execute him just the same ... Refuse to be a courier for the CIA anymore? They would turn him in if he refused. They had a hold on him ... Give Capuchin away to save himself? Impossible. Everyone connected with Capuchin would be put under the hammer. All he could do was find out ... and hope for the best.

He had to be careful. The money the CIA had given him over the years he'd spent gradually. There had been no point in holding on to it. Nor was there any point in banking it. He was encouraged to use the bank, but the bank was just another arm of the KGB. They made periodic checks to see if anyone had more money than they should have. His apartment was

89

comfortable, luxurious by Russian standards; he'd been careful not to make it too luxurious, but all his carefulness would go by the board if the KGB decided to investigate him. It was a pity, he thought, that he didn't live in the West. There, he could spend money without having to watch how much he spent at any one time.

At Schipol airport the plane was waiting for him. As usual, he mused. Always punctual. It would be pretty crowded with passengers but he was always the last to board.

Malin could make out half-a-dozen languages when he boarded, all businessmen trying to obtain contracts with Moscow. But he sat apart; they always did; and his two escorts still did not speak. It was the part of the job he disliked. It wouldn't be so bad if they spoke to him.

Moscow couldn't come soon enough, even if it was only to have a few centimetres of space between himself and the escorts. But within minutes they were cramped against him in another car.

There was still the matter of separating the reports when he arrived at the 2nd Directorate. Each section received reports from different areas of operation, no two sections being allowed to compare their reports. But, somehow, someone managed to read all four. Capuchin did, but how he did was a mystery.

Malin smirked at the ridiculous charade played out when they entered the building housing the directorate. All their fingerprints were taken; they were photographed, weighed and their height measured. How on earth could the Americans substitute someone for him?

The section heads were neither pleased nor sorry to see him. As was normal, they simply took their resp 'ive packages and signed for them, six times, then returning to their desks to study them.

The bloodhounds left Malin then, and somewhat relieved he sought a cup of coffee from one of the bright and gaudy machines dotted around. The coffee tasted vile, but he bought one each time he made a delivery. And it gave him a chance to study Capuchin.

There was no message for him. The desk calendar on Capuchin's desk wasn't positioned the way it would be if there was something for him. Capuchin did nothing unusual. He might not have been aware of his presence. He just leaned over his desk and sorted the reports into small piles.

How, wondered Malin, could he make contact with the Chinese? Moscow and Peking weren't on speaking terms and to be seen with the Chinese was to invite investigation ... How could he find out one way or another? It was virtually impossible. He was a courier. Not a spy.

He had a week's leave due to him before returning to Holland, during which time, he knew, Capuchin might contact him. That was something he didn't want at present.

Only when he was in the open air did Malin realise he was sweating heavily. He hailed a taxi, flashing his KGB credentials to get preferential treatment, and told the driver to take him to the Lenin Hotel. He was there in minutes, and when the taxi screeched to a halt another pulled up behind him.

He could have fainted. God! He uttered the forbidden word. They were on to him already! He threw the driver ten Dutch Guilders and hurried into the hotel bar, aware that the man getting out of the second taxi was Chinese.

The barman, as bored as the taxi-driver had been when he called him, came over only when he growled. He paid through the nose for Scotch, drinking it quickly and pushing the glass forward for another. Then the Oriental came alongside him.

Malin's hand shook when he took the second whisky. He remembered then that there was a deputation from China in Moscow for talks on Vietnam and Cambodia. Everyone in the East was invading everyone else, killing each other by the thousands, then demanding to talk about it.

The hotel had a number of Chinese booked in, too many to count, making it a safe bet that every single one of them was being followed. They wouldn't be able to breathe but it would be noted.

The Oriental ordered a beer, in perfect Russian with a Moscow accent, nudging Malin slightly. Malin trembled. Someone would be watching. He downed his drink quicker than he had the first, dropped some coins on the bar and rushed out. He practically ran back to his apartment.

Behind the comparative safety of the double-locked door he

flung himself into a chair and breathed heavily. His whole body was shaking and his fine silk shirt was soaked with sweat. He stretched out to grasp a bottle of gin, nearly dropping it, and took a long swallow from the open neck.

Why now? He wondered. Why so sudden? Why should the Americans suddenly think Capuchin was working for the Chinese? And the Chinese so suddenly turn up? Events so sudden didn't give him time to think.

He stripped and showered, changed his clothing, emptying the pockets of his suit. Then he found the note.

It hadn't been there when he'd gone into the Lenin. It could only have come from the Oriental – the slight bump at the bar! His fingers trembled while he unfolded it, his eyes widening when he read the message: WE MUST MEET.

His face ballooned, his mouth jammed shut, a whine forming at the back of his throat. Bile tried to find its way out and he wanted to scream.

Gradually he calmed, assisted by the English gin. The telephone rang. He jumped clear of the chair, the bottle landing some way off to drain into the carpet. On wobbly legs he stared at the instrument, willing it to stop, but he knew it wouldn't. If he didn't answer it someone would start banging on the walls. It terrified him.

When he did find the courage to lift the receiver, he had to hold it with both hands.

'Hello …' His voice was hoarse with fear.

·'Comrade Malin,' the voice said; a kind voice. 'I'll speak to you during our evening stroll.'

Stroll! Malin gasped. What stroll? He never took an evening stroll. But the receiver was dead.

Nearly in tears, Malin covered himself in warm clothing. He hoped the telephone wasn't bugged; and hoped no one would recognise him underneath the fur hood.

It was snowing when he reached the street. It was beginning; the long months of snow and freezing cold. Plenty of people were about, all wrapped up to keep out the cold. He joined them, walking slowly as was the custom … there was nothing to rush for. He wanted to look round to see if he was being followed, but for a man in his position that was suspicious.

He walked around for ten minutes, wondering, hoping no one would make contact. It came when he was least expecting it. He was passing a bus queue; they were all bunching ready to board the approaching bus, and he felt the hand go into his pocket.

Going aboard the bus seemed the right thing to do. It was warm, and it gave him the opportunity to put his hand into his pocket. There was another piece of paper with a message on it: TUCHESKAYA STREET 25.

It was only two stops away. He could they have known what route he would take? He didn't want to go, but he had to. He had to know if it was the Chinese.

The bus crawled, making him impatient. Other passengers noticed how much he was shaking. They winked at each other, lifting their thumbs to their mouths in a drinking gesture. He was obviously one of Moscow's many alcoholics.

At Tucheskaya Street he jumped off the bus first and hurried to number 25. He knocked. The door opened, complete darkness behind it, and a hand took him inside. Someone, he could hear them breathing, guided him into a room, and when the light came on his legs gave out. He stumbled, caught himself on a table and lowered himself into a seat. The Oriental was there, the one from the Lenin. How could they have known?

'My name is Koong,' The Oriental said. 'Tsai Koong. We met briefly earlier.'

'Why here?' Malin gasped. 'Why in Moscow? You are being followed!'

'There are ways to outwit the KGB, Comrade Malin.'

'What do you want of me? If I am seen ...'

'We wish to make certain you will be the right man for the job.'

'What job?' Malin could only squeak.

'Recently we lost one of our couriers, Comrade Malin. Your name was given to us as a replacement. We know so much about you ...'

'Capuchin!' Malin was beyond caution.

Koong smiled. 'A most efficient person to have in one's organisation.'

'How? When?'

'It does not matter, comrade; but he is your contact, yes?'

Malin felt himself aging. He couldn't believe it was happening to him. He nodded.

'I will not bore you, comrade, with the consequences that will result if you do not agree to act as my new courier. We will proceed immediately with some details. In future you will make two drops in Rotterdam instead of one. Obviously ...' Koong smiled. 'You will say nothing to the Americans, but you will supply us with identical information.'

'I ... How? ... But ...' Malin croaked.

'You will now tell me in detail your exact movements from when you pick up your information in the Directorate, until you deposit it in Rotterdam. Do not use code-names. I must be certain that your contacts are whom I think they are.'

Malin was trapped. He went through every detail, repeating himself when Koong wasn't sure of a point, and when he gave Capuchin's real name Koong never blinked.

'He was right.' Koong said. 'But I had to make certain. You are the man who will carry out the most important task set by my superiors in Peking. And you will not go unrewarded.' Koong handed over 1,000 US dollars.

Too much! Malin's brain screamed at him. Things were happening too fast.

'We will leave now, my friend.' Koong switched out the light. 'I will go first. And a warning ... Do not speak to your contact about our meeting.'

Koong left, silently disappearing into the cold and snowy night.

Malin's nerves were fraying. In his hand was $1,000, too much to have in his possession. He couldn't spend it in Moscow, nor could he bank it, nor could it be taken out of the country. It was incredible. In a matter of minutes he'd agreed to be an agent of the Chinese ... Why? ... How?

His body began shaking violently, beyond his control. His balance seemed to be upside down. He gripped the table and burst into tears.

Huan was ecstatic when Koong brought him the news. It had been so simple. Five of his men had given out five slips of paper to five couriers. Nothing could have been simpler. One of them, he knew — the culprit — would respond in some way. He would have to respond. He could not be sure if he was being put to task by the KGB during one of its security drills. Fear would do the rest.

Major Zibor Grest was still investigating. Several times he had read through the files of the directors and section heads. So far he had discovered nothing. The conduct of every employee was exemplary. They were all loyal. Yet. ...

He kept searching, and when, as he knew he would, he found what he was looking for he allowed the flicker of a smile to cross his face.

Fifteen

'It's a God-damned disaster!' Rogal spat. 'Capuchin is working for the Chinese Reds.'

Joe Mellini sighed. The trip to London had tired him out.

'Things are going wrong, Ray … Why?'

'How the hell do I know? No one can make head nor tail of anything. Balquidder is behaving as if he hadn't a care in the world.'

'Don't trust him.'

'I don't. But he scares me.'

'And he's scared. He's known Capuchin's identity for some time but has chosen now to tell us, because we know that he has someone in there. He's suggested that Capuchin is a Peking Red to get us off his back.'

'Capuchin will be useless if he is working for the chinks.'

'I know. That's why we've got to find their man … or "V".'

'We've tried twice. We learned nothing and wound up with dead bodies.'

'Balquidder might know.'

'Jeez, chief, we can't lift Balquidder.'

'Ordinarily, no. But this is an emergency. To get the same information as London, we must do anything to find their man.'

'Okay, chief. But we'll be treading on important toes. Balquidder's already warned me off.'

'Fuck Balquidder! I want that man.'

The Vicar received a communication from Kocker. It was short, without explanation. He stared at it for some time: MAKENTOV IS TO VISIT BRITAIN.

96

Erghizh Nijinsky Makentov. A recent article in a Sunday newspaper came to mind. The man the article called Stalin's twin brother — a hardliner. Like Stalin his origins were a little obscure. Believed to be an Armenian born before the First World War, he came to prominence in the years following the revolution. Lenin had taken him onto his staff and given him carte-blanch to protect Mother Russia. He had been ruthless in following orders, a killer. He became Stalin's eyes and ears, and with Stalin was reputed to be responsible for the massacre of an entire race of people in one of the Asian republics. During the purges of the thirties he flourished and — the Vicar recalled Kocker's warning in Berlin — was credited with the imprisonment or death of many who set eyes on the West at the end of the war.

He was old now and no longer held — officially — a position of real importance within the Soviet. No one appeared to be misled however. Although Makentov was officially the General Secretary of the Federation of Russian Trades Unions, it was accepted that he was still a high-ranking member of the KGB.

So he was coming to Britain. The fact that the General Secretary of the Federation of Russian Trades Unions was paying Britain a visit would soon be public knowledge. The visit would be arranged through the Foreign Office and the Press would be informed.

But Kocker was giving him prior notice. Why? There was nothing suspicious about a Russian trade union leader visiting Britain. There had been visits in the past, and reciprocal visits by British trade unionists. In fact, it was a regular occurrence.

The Vicar believed he knew everything there was to know about Makentov. Kocker had supplied him in the past with detailed information on everyone of any note in the Kremlin, and others when they rose through the ranks. Kocker's information wasn't to be questioned. But what was Kocker telling him now, he wondered?

He called Balquidder's office and asked for every scrap of information on Makentov. There must have been something he had missed.

Nothing other than he already knew came back in reply. Makentov, like every member of the Soviet, was firmly ccmputed in his brain. And yet, something had to be missing. Kocker was telling him because it was necessary. There was no explanation, therefore it had to be a warning of some kind.

A warning about what? What was so important about Makentov's visit?

Balquidder drove out to a house on the London-Essex border, a quiet residence he used when his overworked body had reached the limits and cried out for rest. It was late at night when he arrived. The street was quiet. His key slid noiselessly into the front door lock, the distinct click when he turned it telling him that it hadn't been tampered with. Stepping inside he sensed something was wrong, but he was tired, less alert than he should have been. The snout of a muzzled gun was pushed into his face.

'Just don't say anything, Mr Balquidder.' He recognised the American accent. Rogal's people. 'Come in slowly and keep your hands perfectly still.'

Balquidder closed the door with his foot and stepped across the mat.

'Stop!'

Someone patted him for weapons.

'He's clean.'

'My dear sir,' Balquidder said with confidence. 'This is no time for dramatics. Guns are not carried by Her Majesty's Civil Service.'

'No one asked you to speak.' A fist banged into the side of his head.

Balquidder toppled over, pain piercing his head, falling heavily to the floor. Someone kicked him and he grunted with annoyance and renewed pain, but he took the opportunity to take something from his pocket and drop it on the floor.

His eyes were becoming accustomed to the dark. He counted three men, all armed. Two of them pulled him roughly to his feet and pushed their guns into his middle.

'We take your car,' one of them said.

That suited Balquidder.

The street was like a graveyard. Only a handful of lights could be seen coming from the other plush homes, slipping through gaps in curtains. It was ideal for an abduction.

Standard CIA procedure was used getting into the car. One man drove and the other two flanked Balquidder in the back seat, their guns jammed into his ribs. The driver turned the ignition key, unaware as he did so that an alarm began ringing at the local police station.

Balquidder was disappointed after only a few hundred yards. They changed cars, abandoning Balquidder's. Waiting was a German BMW.

'Not particularly patriotic, you chaps.' He dug at them.

'Shut up!' The man on his right said, pushing the gun harder. 'Just give me the excuse and I'll put one in you.'

'You wouldn't dare, old thing. Ray would be terribly upset.'

'Don't this guy give you the shits?' said the other.

'Yeah,' said the driver..' Maybe he needs a smack in the teeth.'

One of the guns came up and Balquidder lost two teeth. Balquidder picked up the two teeth from his lap, put them into his pocket, dabbed his mouth with a handkerchief until the blood stopped flowing, then sat up straight and looked at the road ahead.

'Jesus Christ!' one of the men gasped.

Their destination was a restaurant in Central London, but before they reached the darkened back entrance, Balquidder's people knew who had abducted him. On the alarm signal being sounded a patrol car from the local police station sped to Balquidder's house and found the blue button inside the front door. It was a simple method of communicating. In Balquidder's position abduction by a foreign power was never discounted. One of his pockets always contained a blue button, the other a red, and instant indication of who his abductors might be.

In the restaurant's wine-cellar he was stripped of his clothing and tied to an empty wine rack. Some time passed. His three abductors stood around smoking and talking about nothing in particular. They ignored him. It was cold and he began to feel it.

Rogal came eventually with a man Balquidder hadn't seen before. He was around the forty mark, not too tall but broad and strong. He had a look about him that told Balquidder trouble was coming.

'Welcome to the greasy spoon, Colin,' Rogal smiled. 'I'm sorry we have to do this, but ...' Rogal spread his arms wide in an empty gesture, 'you did force us into it.'

'Before you do anything foolish, Mr Rogal ...' Balquidder left off the familiarities. 'Let me give you fair warning. It is not a threat. But as a spymaster you are finished. Remember those words.'

Rogal shrugged. He'd been threatened a thousand times before.

'This here,' he pointed to the stranger. 'Is Sergeant Homer T Connelly, a past master at extracting information. In 'Nam he never failed to discover what the department wanted to know.'

'Good evening, Mr Connelly.' Balquidder nodded. 'I do hope you realise what you are getting yourself into? This is not Vietnam or the States.'

'The sergeant doesn't say much, Colin. But you will. You will tell me what you know about "V" and your guy in the Kremlin. The sergeant will make you tell me.'

'Don't be foolish, Mr Rogal. It will gain you nothing.'

'We'll see, Colin.' Rogal nodded at Connelly.

Balquidder prepared himself for the pain that was certain to follow. SAS courses were long and involved, covering many fields, one of which was to undergo intensive mental and physical abuse.

Connelly removed his coat and jacket and then opened a small hold-all.

'On your knees,' he said.

The three thugs pulled him to his knees, still tied to the wine rack, but made sure he could not sit on his heels. They pushed him against the upright with his legs astride it, twisting his feet round to the back face. Connelly came with a hammer and 3in nails and laid them by his right leg.

"It's something the sergeant dreamed up in 'Nam, Colin,' Rogal smiled. 'I appreciate that you've probably had some sort of training to withstand levels of pain, so, the sergeant does the opposite. He'll cause you pain all right, and you'll fight it, but the relief that will come with the drug afterwards will make you talk ... Unless you want to tell me beforehand?'

'You're a bloody fool!' Balquidder snapped.

'You asked for it, Colin.'

A telephone was ringing at the American embassy about the same time Rogal motioned for Connelly to proceed. One of Balquidder's people asked that Mellini be informed immediately that a dim view was being taken over Balquidder's abduction. If Mellini wished to help Anglo-American relations, he would instruct Rogal to release Balquidder at once.

It shook Mellini when word reached him. He was waiting to hear from Rogal. How the English could have known so quickly was incredible. They weren't supposed to know. But they did and that spoiled everything. They couldn't hold Balquidder with the English knowing. He called the restaurant and ordered the operation to be aborted at once.

Connelly was quick. While the others held Balquidder's feet he hammered nails into his soles, driving them hard through the instep and into the wooden upright of the wine-rack. Balquidder's lungs expelled air in long gasps as the nails went in. The pain wasn't too bad, like thumps, but seconds later conditions changed. Blood flowed profusely, then the air reached the wounds. Balquidder screamed. He pushed against his knees, arched his back, strained against the ropes and tried to tear his feet from the nails. The nails pulled and the screams came louder, but now with a touch of hoarseness.

Connelly went back to his hold-all, took out a prepared syringe, tested it then waited for Rogal's command. Rogal showed no compassion. He simply stared at Balquidder. He'd seen it before and knew just how long it could go on. On the command Connelly jabbed the needle into Balquidder's arm. Nothing happened at first. Balquidder continued to scream; veins in his arms and legs rose out of his flesh like bloodstained ropes, then after a minute his body began to relax. His scream was cut off suddenly, plunging the cellar into an eerie silence. He fell back against the upright.

While Balquidder was relaxing Connelly gently lifted his feet off the nails. The nails were not flat-headed and the task was easy, but Balquidder's feet were swollen to twice their normal size. He laid Balquidder flat out on the floor, washed the wou nds with a solution, stitched them up and wrapped them expertly with medical bindings.

Balquidder couldn't understand what was happening to him. Rogal was leaning over him and he knew that he was going to answer any questions truthfully. He knew he shouldn't, but something told him that he would.

'Now then, Colin.' Rogal spoke softly into his ear. 'Tell me about your organisation.'

Balquidder muttered something that Rogal couldn't make sense of. But Rogal was patient. He stroked Balquidder's forehead.

'Tell me about it, Colin. Get it off your chest and you'll feel better.'

'Branch of the Secret Service ...'

'Who gives you your instructions, Colin? Who is your controller?'

'... comes from "V".'

'That's the boy, Colin ... Who is "V"?'

'... don't know ... no one ... knows ...'

'Colin, baby! Someone must know who he is.'

'... don't know ... no one knows ...'

They were interrupted by someone from the restaurant upstairs. Rogal was angry at being disturbed, but after a hurried conversation with the visitor he turned pale.

'For Christ sake get him dressed.' He began to pick up Balquidder's clothes. 'The God-damn limeys know we've got him!'

Rogal was clearly shaken but he made a last attempt to get information. 'Colin!' His voice wasn't so soft. 'Who is your man in the Kremlin?'

'No one knows ...' Balquidder suddenly yelped with pain.

'Too late,' said Connelly. 'Pain's coming back. He'll be no good to you that way.'

Rogal stood. 'Get him out of here – fast!'

He had failed. He watched the three men carry Balquidder from the cellar then sat down and bit his nails. Had he obtained the information things would have been all right. The British would have accepted that Balquidder had talked; he'd be no good to them then; he'd be put out to grass or behind a desk and nothing more would have been said. But he'd ballsed it up. Balquidder had told him nothing, and torturing a senior British Intelligence officer, with no result, wouldn't go down well in either London or Washington. Every man-jack in British Intelligence would be after his hide.

Balquidder was found alongside a telephone kiosk close to Victoria Station. He was blue with cold and unrecognisable. Late-night revellers passed him by, walking around him with disgust. He had to take it all until a police patrol car stopped to pick him up. A telephone call and twenty minutes brought one of his staff to the police station, and under the cloak of the Official Secrets Act he was whisked away to a private hospital.

The Vicar was furious. As soon as Balquidder was able to talk they conversed by telephone.

'What did you tell them, Colin?'

'That my controller was "V".'

'Anything else?'

'Nothing.'

'Can you be sure?'

'I can recall vividly everything that happened. I felt a compulsion to tell him anything he wanted to know. Before he could really get going he was interrupted.'

'Just as well. I've heard that certain departments wish to pursue the matter.'

'I wouldn't, sir.'

'I agree, Colin. Our American friends will expect that, so, that's what we mustn't do.'

'Very good, sir.'

'Get all your people out of sight. Close down for a while.'

The Vicar was a little worried. Washington was stirring up too much dirt.

Sixteen

The closing down of Balquidder's department sent a shockwave through Washington. Rogal had shut himself away in Grosvenor Square, afraid to show himself. The Ambassador waited on a knife-edge for the telephone call that would summon him to Whitehall. In Washington the President waited for a similar call from the British Embassy, knowing he was going to be at a loss for words. The CIA had committed an unpardonable mortal sin. They waited for the British to get their revenge.

No call arrived at the White House, nor at Grosvenor Square. It took the President by surprise; nothing was being said. He issued orders to the reverse. It would be unethical at least, not to own up to the hit.

Sir Alan Bunting received the call at the Home Office and, as was the suggestion of the Secret Service, he duly accepted the invitation to dine at Grosvenor Square. The Ambassador was visibly shaken, and when Sir Alan assumed an air of friendship and joviality it shook the Ambassador even more. Rogal sat with them, instructed to own up at the right moment and convey his sincere apologies, afraid to look at Sir Alan.

'We owe you our apologies, Sir Alan.'

'Oh? For what, old chap?'

'The terrible error we made the other day.'

'Dropped a clanger, did you?'

It was the kind of needling Rogal didn't like. He'd had enough of it from Balquidder.

'You must appreciate that we are embarrassed by it all, Sir Alan.'

'I'm afraid you've got the better of me, old chap. Are you

trying to tell me you've been doing something naughty?'

'All right, Sir Alan. It doesn't have to be rubbed in, you know. I'm shaking here trying to apologise. If there's anything we can—'

'I'm sure I don't know what you're talking about, old chap.'

Rogal couldn't hold back. He was beginning to despise this trait in the English. He wanted it out in the open, over with.

'We're talking about Balquidder!' he all but shouted.

'Balquidder?' Sir Alan was calm, his lips pursed. 'Name rings a bell, but can't quite place it.'

'He's in Intelligence,' said the Ambassador. 'Unfortunately some of our people hurt him rather badly.'

'I would have heard about that.'

'You haven't?'

'No, sir. Perhaps your people made a mistake with identities?'

'You deny it's happened?'

'I can assure you that nothing of that sort has happened to my knowledge for many a year.'

Both Rogal and the Ambassador stopped in mid-swallow. They'd nearly killed Balquidder and the whole thing was being officially denied. It threw them. Neither pursued the subject and dined in silence, both watching Sir Alan to try and understand the denial. It didn't make sense.

After dinner the Ambassador journeyed to an office run by MI6 and met General West, practically begging the General to listen to his confession. West shook his head. Nor did he know anything about someone being badly hurt by their American colleagues.

He hurried back to Grosvenor Square and called Washington. To his amazement he learned that over lunch the British Ambassador had sworn to the President that nothing of the sort had happened. Balquidder was apparently on graduated leave.

'What the hell!' The President barked into his end of the line. 'What in God's name are they playing at?'

After a week of inactivity from Balquidder's department, Joe Mellini made his presence known in London. He had been keeping out of sight but things were happening – or not happening – that he didn't understand. He'd had a week and hadn't come up with anything. Yet he believed the answer was staring him in the face. He tried to contact Balquidder through the Home Office but was told that Balquidder was abroad on vacation. They'd gladly pass on any message he wished to leave.

Balquidder was no more out of the country than he was, Mellini knew. He was hiding somewhere and recovering. He'd taken punishment and was out of the way – as was his whole department. Which meant, Mellini hoped, they were scared. The idea wasn't new to him. It came to him every day. The more he thought about it the more it appealed to him. If London had a route straight into the Kremlin, she had nothing to worry about. But if Rogal had got close without knowing she would be forced to drop out of sight for a while.

Major Zibor Grest delayed his intended visit to Balquidder when he learned of the behind-the-scenes conflict in London. Instead he once again studied the files of the four section heads of the 2nd Directorate of External Planning, paying a great deal of attention to Pytor Janos, aged thirty-seven and youngest of the four section heads. Janos had come to the directorate from the Foreign Ministry and was one of the Kremlin's so-called whizz-kids. He had an uncanny ability to pick up a foreign language in a matter of days. Apparently all he required was the origin of the basic roots of foreign grammar and the rest came naturally. He was married with three children and his wife worked at the Foreign Ministry still, where they first met. He had never been to the West but had met many foreigners. He was popular with them because he could speak to so many in their own language.

Janos lived by routine. Every morning at 07.30 he left the family's smart apartment in the south of the city and drove into the centre. His position entitled him to the use of a car, but not a driver, his wife with the same entitlement. On reaching the office he signed in. Directorate security searched him, took his fingerprints and X-rayed the lining of his attaché case, by which time it was 08.00 and time to begin working. From

08.00 until 08.30 he met with his section supervisors and discussed the morning's mail, delegating each to a specific area of operation. At 08.40 he gathered the work together from the previous day, took it to the Director, then returned to his office to drink his first coffee of the day.

The remainder of the morning was used up by continually checking on the section's clerks, pointing out errors in translation; generally making certain that everyone was carrying out their duties according to procedure. He lunched in the Directorate restaurant from 12.30 until 13.30, always sitting at the same table as his Director and one other section head. Then until 15.00 he assessed the security performance of those in his section, completing the statutory forms for the same. From 15.00 until 16.00 he supervised, and the final hour supervised the locking up of all documents.

Janos moved about his section, Grest noted. He made lots of contact with his people and would notice anything suspicious — or should. But, would any of his section notice anything suspicious about him? Although Janos was a model for communism, there was no reason why he couldn't be a traitor. It could be anyone.

Mirek Ternev was much older, sixty-three and due for retirement, but he was made of sterner stuff than Janos. A war veteran, like many others in government departments, he had graduated to the Directorate from a NKVD fighting division. He had seen action in Poland during the push West; and later, again in Poland, and in Hungary and Czechoslovakia at the time of the riots organised by Western imperialists. An injury in Prague following the quelling of that particular riot forced him to leave military service. He had been a director, but managed to get himself drunk one night some years before, shouting about his years of service with the NKVD and KGB, and consequently was demoted to section head. It had upset him at the time, but eventually he settled down and ran his section efficiently.

No one slacked in his section. Everyone did a full eight hours work each day and if for any reason they did not they were obliged to stay behind in the evening until the eight hours were completed. No one from another section or another directorate was allowed to set foot in his section without first having had his permission. The fact that a member of the Supreme Soviet might have despatched a messenger to him had no influence on his decision. If Ternev thought the reason for the visit was unimportant, the messenger was refused admission.

Unlike Janos, who was a family man, Ternev had never married, but he'd had several women in his time. His present mistress was a young cypher clerk in his own section who, internal security knew, did not like him over much, but clung to him because he had access to the special shops set aside for high-ranking party members. Without realising it, he was doing the KGB a favour. The woman was to be approached with the view to becoming a sex-spy. She had all the qualities if she could fool Ternev.

Although he kept a tight rein on his section, Ternev could not be eliminated from suspicion. He drank often and each time he drank a report was made. Ternev would undoubtedly be aware of this and, if still secretly annoyed over his demotion, could be using his strict routine as a cover for spying.

He saw his mistress on three nights during the week and on Saturday night when they stayed together at his apartment. Each Sunday morning he took her to one of the special shops, buying her some small item from the West. Generally it was a pair of panties or nylons, but now and again he bought her a dress or woollen sweater. On other evenings, or anytime he was not with his mistress or watching sport, he drank. He kept out of the public eye, using the special relaxation centre supplied. So far as security reports showed, he never made contact with anyone from the West; just his mistress and the bottle. But people with even less of a social life had turned out to be Western spies.

Karol Zobovic also had a mistress. Officially there was no such thing as mistresses; immorality was frowned upon by the state and at lower levels in the party, or outside the party, it was regarded as a crime. But within the upper and high levels it was allowed to go on. The echelons saw it as a reward for hard work, subsequently Zobovic's liaison was looked on favourably by security. At forty-nine he was ready to marry again. Ten years earlier it was discovered that his wife's grandfather had been Jewish. Being a conscientious member of the party he divorced her instantly. There was a scandal at the time for it should have been on record about his wife's grandfather's origins. It caused the imprisonment of several respected people in the research department.

His own history was impeccable. A brilliant scholar at college he was earmarked for the directorate long before his graduation. He entered as a senior clerk, jumping over many who'd had several years experience. Everything came to easily and after ten years was promoted to supervisor. Five years later he became section head, and it was taken for granted that he would be a Director by his fiftieth birthday.

His working day was the same as the other section heads. At lunch he sat with Marya Lus, the woman who was to be his second wife. He had an official car, and apartment, spent his vacations on the Baltic coast in the German Democratic Republic, the last four of which with Marya Lus. Off-duty was always spent with Marya, an arrangement that pleased security.

Marya Lus was a section head in the 1st Directorate and divorced. She had been happy in the early years of her marriage, but where her career boomed her husband's failed. He had been thought to be a man with brains but failed the examinations for entry into the Directorate. He now worked as a foreman in a factory making machine-tools.

Marya had been taken to one side and advised to divorce him. They were incompatible by profession; a weak husband could only damage her career, she was told. She protested at first but eventually was persuaded that it was the correct course of action to take. The divorce was pushed quickly through the civil courts.

For a while she was unhappy, told not to remarry until a full year had passed, and then perhaps marry someone the Directorate thought applicable. During the year she met Zobovic. There were thirteen years difference in their ages but they found a genuine love in each other. They forgot their previous spouses but did not marry after the year. The lived apart while Marya worked her way to section head. Now their marriage was due. They were happy and the Directorate was happy; it was good to have two people of the same profession and intellect as husband and wife.

But … either of them could be a spy. What could be better cover than to marry someone favoured by the Directorate? One of them could talk in their sleep, or one could get the other to talk about their work. People in love sometimes said things they lived to regret.

Alexi Gagarin – the Man of Iron – had lived for several years in the West as a trade official. He had made it known that he liked London as a posting more than anywhere else. He used English like an Englishman and anything English stocked in the special shops he bought at any price. But he was no traitor, according to security. A Russian patriot to the core. As a trading official he had never given in to the West's connivance to sell them goods cheap just because they were made in Russia. He struck the hardest of bargains, taking as much as he could get and giving as little as he could in return. He never failed. He was sixty now. A younger man had taken his place and he was content to work out his remaining years as a section head in the Directorate. He had made many contacts in the West, a number of whom were now working for him as minor agents, mostly in the field of industrial espionage. They fed him information not classified under Western official secrets, but regarded as vital to the West's technological advancement. In some cases the information was more valuable than secret information. It meant that Russia could manufacture modern aids without incurring the massive initial costs of research and development.

Like Ternev he was a hard taskmaster. One single cup of coffee first thing in the morning was all that was allotted to his staff, and woe-betide anyone who attended the toilets more than twice during their eight hours. He insisted that everyone address each other by their security number rather than by name. Names, he contended, bred familiarity, and he wanted no familiarity in his section. They were there to work.

He lunched alone, always sitting by a window in the same seat every day. No one had yet taken his seat by mistake. While eating his eyes never left his food, and afterwards, until a minute before the end of the lunch break, he watched the people in the street below through the double-glazing.

Out of work he was a different person. A grandfather, he doted on his three grandchildren. Before going home every night he stopped off at the homes of his two daughters, leaving two bars of English chocolate at one, and one bar at the other.

Again he had perfect cover. His liking for England and his love for Mother Russia could be false. It could be the other way round. The uniqueness of his open declaration of liking England being accepted, could be a factor completely fooling security and the Soviet. No one else could make a statement like it and continue in a high position.

Although Grest admired them all, doubt appeared. They had worked hard to earn their luxuries. But any of them could be a traitor. It was always those you trusted who turned out to be rotten.

The President, Joe Mellini and Rogal felt it. There was something wrong with London's reaction to the incident with Balquidder. They had fallen over themselves to apologise and make amends, but the British were behaving as if nothing had happened. It made them look and feel foolish and the British would know how they felt.

London knew the identity of Capuchin. They hadn't given him away – and weren't likely to for it would damage relations to an irreparable extent. But they were behaving oddly. Washington would never rest until the identities of both 'V' and Prairie Dog were known; London could protect Prairie Dog by giving away Capuchin; it appeared that Capuchin was the only lead to Prairie Dog, yet London seemed uninterested in him. It didn't make sense. London was keeping a low profile, more or less inviting them to discover Prairie Dog's identity, standing to one side while it happened.

Which was suspicious. One could never fathom the working mind of the British.

Seventeen

In Lisbon, CIA agent James Rift drank his daily half-dozen in the small tavern alongside the river. Every weekday at exactly 12.30 he arrived at the tavern, sat at the same table on the pavement, lunched on the same amount of cheese, tomatoes and bread, and drank six small glasses of wine. He was a regular customer and having used the tavern for two years was regarded as part of the local scenery.

The fact that he was a CIA agent was well known to the authorities and to the Intelligence services of other countries. But since he seemed to trouble no one, no great amount of interest was taken in him. He was believed to be a minor employee of the CIA, a courier and contact-man. Russia and Great Britain however, knew him to be the director-general for the Iberian peninsula.

Between 12.30 and 13.30 various people stopped at his table and spoke for a few seconds then left. Rift continued his lunch. When his lunch was over he walked the half mile to the office of PORTA-US EXPORT INCORPORATED, there taking charge of the CIA-sponsored company employing Portuguese nationals.

The day he didn't arrive back at his office was well planned. A series of events led up to the day, events that were both devious and clever. Several days before, Theres Duarte, a receptionist at the British Embassy, told her lover, one Babtista Oliveira, that an infernal row was going on between the English and Americans. The English had an agent high in the Kremlin.

'And the Americans are offended?' Baptista said.

'Yes, apparently they feel they should have first call on any information coming from Russia.'

'No one knows who he is?'

'That's right. They are fighting each other. All the American residentés have been told to listen for information.'

'Does Moscow know about this agent in the Krelin?'

'They have no idea that he is there. He is so high up that no one will suspect him.'

'You think there might be information to be had here, in Lisbon?'

'The English think that the CIA residenté here will have been told.'

'Interesting,' said Baptista, rising from the bed. 'Go back to work, Theres. I must go and report.'

The prospect excited Baptista. Lisbon had been comparatively quiet since the Salazar regime ended. There had been plenty of riots and protest marches since then, but there had been more intrigue and double-dealings while Salazar was in power. Communism was banned then and affairs were conducted in secret. But now with everything in the open it was less exciting. The popular liberation committee needed something to get its teeth into and this could be it.

The PLC, the only political party banned since the coming of democracy, had few members, but they were scattered around in important locations. Baptista Oliveira held a responsible position with an American oil company and every single item of company business he passed on to Moscow. Others worked in various government departments, some for other governments, all acting as couriers.

No one really took the PLC seriously. There were several communist parties in the country, all of them now legal, but the PLC was banned because it preached revolution to win power. During the political turmoil following Salazar's death its pamphlets swamped the country urging people to take up arms and remove those who had oppressed them for so many years. A few guns were fired but the armed revolutionaries were quickly caught and put to death. Portugal had been lucky. There had been no civil war or armed struggle when power was taken from the Salazar politicians; a government elected by the people came into power.

Where before the PLC had organised and administered opposition to the regime, it was now cast aside, scorned, thrown onto the scrap heap as an inefficient and unpatriotic organisation. Its numbers dropped until it could no longer be termed a political party, for a while disappearing into obscurity.

Moscow didn't forget them. They were the ultra-left, the hard-line communists who never gave up. They were used as spies. They kept watch on foreign businessmen and politicians, on foreign investment and trade, reporting on other political parties. They also did any dirty jobs that came along.

Baptista was part of the executive committee, Theres one of his agents. Both were sworn to secrecy and having Theres installed as a receptionist was one of the biggest coups they had carried off. Theres was a wealth of information. The English seemed so haphazard with whom they shared their information with. It was a standing joke that the receptionist knew more than the Ambassador himself.

The executive met and discussed the friction between London and Washington. It was an important event when the two leading Western powers fell out, something not to be treated lightly. The discussion lasted several hours and an agreement was reached. The executive would take steps to realise a dream. When Moscow learned of their success they would be given what they had always wanted – control of the communist parties affiliated to the socialists in government. Then things would change.

As the church clock struck the half-hour that day, James Rift paid his bill, added the usual generous tip, waved to the tavern-owner's wife and strolled back to the office of PORTA-US. The weather was still fine; he was glad not to be in Washington where it would be cold. He stopped at the kerb, waiting for the traffic to clear, when a small English car pulled up in front of him. Three men were inside, one driving and two in the back. The driver leaned over, opened the front passenger door and called out to him.

'Please get in, Mr Rift.'

Rift saw the silenced gun pointed at him from the back seat and obeyed, the car immediately speeding away from the kerb. He smiled. Whoever they were would be in for a shock when

114

they realised who he worked for.

The car raced out of Lisbon, breaking all speed laws, driving non-stop until it reached a villa on the outskirts of Torres Jedras, a town twenty miles from the capital. The villa was run-down; it had large gardens overrun with weeds, but the high fence surrounding it was in excellent condition.

More than a dozen people were in the villa, men and women. Rift was surprised to be introduced to the chairman of the PLC, Dr Antonio Louro. Louro was polite, but his intentions were obvious and wasted no time.

'We are anxious to know about the disagreement between your organisation and the British Secret Service, Mr Rift. We are aware that London has a spy highly placed in the Kremlin; that your people would like to know his identity. We would like to know just how much you know.'

Rift chuckled. 'You can't be serious. Even Moscow would think twice before lifting someone in my position.'

'We are perfectly serious, Mr Rift.'

'Hell, Doctor. You're out of your league. Don't be a God-damned fool!'

Rift hadn't met Louro before, but he knew of him. Louro was getting on, in his late fifties, a medium-sized guy with gold-rimmed glasses and silver hair. He'd dropped out of politics when democracy arrived. Previously he'd been a bitter opponent of Salazar, spending some years in prison for his troubles, yet when the chance to make a name for himself arrived he didn't take it. So far as everyone was aware, he was just a respectable man lecturing in European history at the university. The CIA knew however that he was still a Stalinist.

'Mendro ...' Louro said quiety.

Tomas Mendro, a young student, pushed Rift into a chair and pointed a silenced gun at him.

'We wish to know everything you know about the situation, Mr Rift.' Louro said.

Rift shook his head. 'Don't meddle, Doctor.'

Mendro shot Rift in the right elbow. Bone splinters and blood splashed several feet and Rift screamed with pain. His arm, useless, fell and hung by the side of the chair.

'We will do the same to your other arm, Mr Rift ... Can you

imagine what it will be like not to have the use of your arms?'

Rift didn't have to have it spelled out for him. He talked. He told Louro everything he knew about the London/Washington feud.

'Thank you, Mr Rift.' Louro smiled. 'Now we will attend to your arm and send you on a trip.'

Five hours later a large packing case arrived at Portela international airport, ready for shipment to Moscow under diplomatic baggage.

It was not unusual for Louro to despatch packing cases full of documents and it was quickly taken into the hangar serving Aeorflot, where the necessary diplomatic labels were stuck to it. Breathing through the air holes in the side was a heavily drugged James Rift.

The packing case was carefully loaded into a giant Ilyushin jet-liner re-routed for the purpose, but it wasn't until the jet was over Soviet air-space that the case was opened. The KGB members of the crew were astonished. Why the resident CIA official in Lisbon was lying inside was a mystery; there had been no forewarning. Louro's report was read and Moscow radioed.

The information was given to Major Grest who, when he read through the report, drove hard to Domodedovo airport. His face was ashen and lines of worry creased his normally smooth forehead. He desperately hoped that the information was wrong, a mistake. He was beside himself while he waited for the jet to land, both furious and frightened. When the jet did touch down he had to be restrained from dashing out to the craft before it taxied to a halt.

Quickly the packing case was transferred to a sealed off building and the cover removed. Grest gasped. He knew by sight every CIA residenté. Before him was undoubtedly one James Rift.

An ambulance came and whisked Rift to a KGB hospital and given into the care of skilled surgeons. Grest used the room next door to study the report from Louro.

He could hardly believe it. It was incredible. A man with more standing in diplomatic circles than the American Ambassador himself, kidnapped and shot by Soviet agents!

'How? Why?' The Chairman of the Supreme Soviet demanded later. 'Who issued the order?'

'I certainly did not,' Grest protested. 'Lisbon hadn't even been told.'

'What about the woman?'

'A trusted member of the Lisbon group.'

'Louro acted on his own?'

'He must have. His orders were solely to collect information until the time to intercede arrived.'

'You realise what you've done, Major?'

What he had done, thought Grest. He hadn't known anything about it.

'I will take steps to put the matter right.'

'You know we can't give him back?'

Grest nodded.

'Louro,' the Chairman went on, 'is no longer useful to us.'

Again Grest nodded. That was evident.

Grest left the hurriedly-called Supreme Soviet still frightened. There was no way they could explain themselves to the Americans. They could only hope that no one noticed. Rift could be sent back with a smashed arm and tell everyone that Moscow was sorry, that it was a mistake. No one would believe that. Rift would have to be killed and his body made to disappear. He would be drained of information of course, but what they'd done could not be undone. And if the Americans ever found out ...

It destroyed years of hard work. As collectors of information Louro and his executive were excellent. Louro had someone everywhere that mattered in Portugal. In time they would have taken over and Russia would have been given a base in the North Atlantic.

Now it was destroyed. Louro and his exective could not be allowed to carry on working. Sooner or later someone would give away what they had done and Moscow would be in deep trouble. There were things that just were not done; kidnapping the resident agent of a foreign Intelligence service was one of them.

At least, thought Grest, it verified his own knowledge of the situation. Rift had told Louro that the CIA had a spy highly placed in the Kremlin, but not so highly placed as a British spy. The CIA was naturally worried. But what made the situation worse was the frightening admission by Rift that the CIA spy might also be working for the Chinese.

An assassination squad from Angola entered Portugal only two days later to begin the task of executing every member of the PLC's executive, but not before Theres Duarte had reported her part in the kidnapping to the director of Intelligence at the British Embassy. Louro had reacted as expected.

Intelligence was more than pleased. An account was despatched immediately to London with an assurance that all evidence would be disposed of. London would not be connected in any way.

They would have to find a replacement for Theres Duarte.

The same day an anonymous letter arrived at the American Embassy informing the ambassador of James Rift's kidnapping, by a group of terrorists in the pay of Moscow. The plane, flight number, the captain's name and the cargo were mentioned. It went without saying that enquiries would show the information to be genuine. Washington would then be hammering on Moscow's door for an explanation.

Eighteen

Capuchin didn't notice the Oriental following him. If he had, he wouldn't have been too perturbed. There were many Orientals in Moscow, from the far eastern republics and from the Peoples Republic of Mongolia. They were part of the Moscow scenery.

Washington would have to know that Grest was investigating him. He would have to tell them that no more information would be forthcoming until Grest had finished. In one sense it worried Capuchin, in another he felt safe with the knowledge that he was well hidden. Nonetheless, no chances could be taken.

Koong kept a respectful distance. He had not dressed in the regulatory Chinese dress of quilted jacket and trousers, but in a costume peculiar to the area of Tannou Touva in the east. He mingled easily with the crowds walking the pavements, virtually disappearing in the sea of faces when he walked down the steps of the Metro.

He paid the few kopecks that were the standard fare and stayed behind Capuchin. No one took any notice of him, least of all the police; they were too busy rounding up the drunks trying to sleep it off in the warm coaches of the trains. Capuchin wasn't as agitated as his courier, he noticed. Capuchin was perfectly calm, confident, sure of himself.

Capuchin was thinking of Malin. Only Malin and their controller knew of them and Malin could be relied on. It was a simple matter of informing Malin that communications would be severed for a time while the investigations were going on. Malin would know what to do; he had done it before when Grest appeared in the Directorate.

He could do with a rest. It wasn't always easy feeding

119

intormation to the CIA. It took a tremendous amount of nerve to commit treason knowing what the consequences would be if he were caught. A rest would do him a world of good.

Capuchin rode four stations and got off the train. He neither looked right nor left, but strode up the steps into the dark street with a purpose. He crossed the road, heading for an old, darkened, boarded-up entrance to a shop. It still had its former Jewish owner's name above the painted window. It was a precaution he always took. When he met with Malin he had to be doubly careful that security wasn't following him.

He watched the remainder of the people disgorge themselves from the sloping tunnel. They too had a purpose. It was extremely cold and snowing; no one had a great desire to stay out too long. Several Orientals were among them.

Koong came from the exit and stopped at the kerb to pull up his collar. Its thick fur lining hid his face. He watched for traffic, crossed the road and stood by the bus stop. From the bus stop he could view the length of the pavement for several hundred yards on either side of the Metro station.

It didn't worry him that he couldn't see Capuchin. Capuchin could not just vanish. He waited. The crowds from the Metro disappeared and the only people in the street were local stragglers. Some entered the station, then only its bright lights were there. He waited still further. A movement caught his eye.

Koong didn't change his stance. He continued to beat his gloved hands together, but watched the hunched figure come from the darkened doorway at the same time. It was Capuchin without a doubt. Koong smiled. The man was good. He waited until Capuchin was well on his way before following.

Capuchin left the main thoroughfare, turning off suddenly into a side-street. His footprints were behind him in the snow. Koong didn't have to hurry. Capuchin turned another corner into a brightly lit square, where people were piling from another Metro station. He never used the station, although he could have; but too many people he knew would be using it and he didn't want to meet them.

The crowd filed in one direction, to the ice-hockey stadium nearby. Capuchin took the opposite direction, to a sports palace where a gymnastic competition was to be played. He joined the queue, stamping his feet like the others.

When the doors opened there was a solid surge as the queue rushed to get into the warmth. Capuchin joined them, carried along by those behind, paid his ten kopecks and entered the arena. He managed to get his usual seat, right behind the tunnel where the gymnasts came out. It was perfect there. Malin and he could lean over the protecting wall and talk without being overheard.

The young gymnasts came out, limbering-up for the evening's competition. Malin was nowhere in sight; if he didn't hurry someone would take his seat and they wouldn't be able to demand it back.

Someone sat beside him, coughed, then gently tapped twice against the protecting wall. Capuchin didn't look round but sighed with relief. He paid attention to the announcer's comments. The competition was to be between the Soviet Union's Olympic squad and a team from the German Democratic Republic.

The competition began and he joined in the applause for the first gymnasts. Then he turned his head slightly and saw the elbows on top of the wall and grunted with disappointment. The hands at the end of the coat sleeves were not Malin's. It was a wasted journey. He leaned back, intending to look round to see if Malin had arrived late.

He became alert. Something about the Oriental beside him was familiar. He did not come into contact with Orientals at work or socially. He'd met some in the past when the two countries were on speaking terms, but the man next to him was not one of them. Yet, he knew he'd seen him before ... one of Grest's men?

He couldn't stay. If it was Grest's man he would have to leave; but it would be wrong to leave suddenly. Screwing his eyes shut, his hand went up to his forehead, making a show of having developed a headache. His head shook a couple of times and he felt round his eyes. He bared his teeth, pressing into his forehead with his thumbs, and made to rise.

'Don't leave yet, Comrade Capuchin.'

Capuchin froze. He could sense the lips inches from his ear; there was a hand laid gently on his knee. Looking through his fingers he saw the Oriental quite plainly.

'Please lean forward as you do with Comrade Malin,' Koong said.

Capuchin obliged, his eyes glued to the arena. His body became weak.

At the back of the crowd Nikolai Malin stood, breathless. He cursed the two Orientals who'd bumped into him. They'd insisted on brushing down his coat, inspecting it to make sure they hadn't damaged it. It caused him to miss his train and the fact that they were Chinese frightened him. At first he thought they came from Koong, but eventually they left him alone. But he'd missed the train and the seats at the arena were taken up quickly. He'd run all the way from the station, gasping when he reached the arena. When he spotted Koong beside Capuchin he nearly cried out with terror.

It was true! ... Capuchin was working for Peking ... It was all true!

Malin panicked. He turned and ran pell-mell down the stairs into the street, pushing his way past the arena's director, causing the man to stumble and fall. He ran across the square, caution thrown to the wind, into the Metro station. The ticket seller gazed with amazement when he threw down several coins and grabbed a ticket. No one overpaid if they could help it.

He fidgeted and sweated on the train. His hands shook and his bottom lip trembled with fear. Capuchin had gone too far. It was bad enough spying for the CIA, but spying for Peking at the same time was a thousand times worse. He experienced some of the terror others experienced when they were taken into a court charged with treason. It was indescribeable. The Soviet Government had no equal when it came to instilling terror into a person. The thought of being interrogated by KGB experts horrified him.

Malin drank himself into a stupor when he arrived back in his apartment, hoping that the next day there would be a trip to the West. If there was, he would go with pleasure. Then promptly defect to the Americans.

The director of the gymnastic arena was not accustomed to people causing him to fall to the ground, particularly when they should have known that to be in his position he had to be a loyal party member. No one could abuse a party member and get away with it.

He called the civil police, gave a fairly accurate description of the man. He did not know the man's name but recognised him as a frequent visitor. The man was acting suspiciously – people in Moscow did not run – like a criminal. Yet he was very well dressed.

The circumstances were sufficient for the KGB to be contacted.

'Who am I?' Koong replied to the question before it was asked. 'I am Tsai Koong, a representative of the People's Republic of China holding diplomatic immunity.' Koong produced an identity card issued by the KGB, showing it briefly to Capuchin. 'I am your new controller.'

Capuchin continued to stare at the competition. It was all a bad dream.

'I know all about you, Comrade Capuchin. Does that not put you in a difficult position?'

Capuchin began to shake. He couldn't stop it. Initially his mind was wondering if Koong was what he claimed to be, or if he was a plant of Grest's. But the mention of his code-name wiped both out. Someone knew him and it didn't matter if it was Moscow or Peking.

'We have things to discuss, Comrade Capuchin.'

'Don't call me that!' Capuchin hissed.

'What should I call you, comrade?'

'What do you want?'

'I wish to employ your services, comrade.'

'Don't be stupid.'

'I offer you riches, comrade.'

'Money?' Capuchin looked round sharply. 'What good is money in Moscow?'

'I want you to continue as normal, Comrade. I want you to continue to give information to Comrade Malin, your courier, but I want you to supply him with answers to questions I will ask of him.'

'It can't be done.'

'But, indeed it can. It is a simple matter of priorities. You either work for me as I say, or you do not work for anyone at all.'

Capuchin sagged. There was no way of getting out of it.

'It won't be easy. You don't know what it involves getting out what I can now ... and there is an investigation going on.'

'One risk is no bigger than another, Comrade. Obviously you will wait until the investigation ends before commencing our relationship.'

Capuchin nodded. He had no choice. Koong got up.

'Do not attempt to cheat me, Comrade Capuchin. If I learn that you have, you will be met one day in the street by one of my people ... right under the eyes of the KGB.'

Capuchin trembled, not stopping until long after Koong left the arena. He stayed until the competition was over, remembering nothing about it. On reaching home he lay in bed until the early hours of the morning wondering how the Chinese managed to get on to him.

Next morning Malin reported to his superior and asked if he was due to leave that day for Holland. No, his superior shook his head. There was a breach of security and all external services were suspended while the investigations were going on. Malin could have extended leave while it lasted.

Malin left with his mouth and throat parched. His head ached. He had a terrible job trying to keep his hands from shaking. He badly needed a drink. He was trapped. They didn't know ... but they would eventually ... there was no way he could get out.

Capuchin's state was noticeable when he arrived at work. He looked extremely tired, his eyes dark around the edges. He was unshaven and hadn't changed his clothes from the previous day.

'Are you feeling unwell, Comrade?' His director asked.

Capuchin nodded. 'I feel terrible.'

'Why did you not stay at home?'

'Thought I might brighten up as the day went on.'

'Tch, Comrade. We can't have someone in your position coming to work ill, eh! You could make mistakes.'

'Should I go home?'

'Of course. You are too valuable to be ill. I will have a car come for you. Stay in bed for a day or two.'

'Thank you Comrade Director.'

Capuchin couldn't settle when he got home. He paced the floor trying to fathom out how the Chinese found him and Malin. Only two men in Washington knew who he was and they certainly wouldn't have spoken out of turn.

He couldn't contact Malin. They had a strict rule that they met only at the arena and Malin wouldn't go there until their next meeting was due. He daren't telephone; Malin wouldn't telephone him, and if Malin was thinking what he was thinking, Malin would be a very worried man.

Nineteen

'It's all over bar the shouting, Colin,' the Vicar told Balquidder by telephone.

Balquidder was mending fast. The nails had missed vital veins and bones and the wounds were healing over and he was able to get about with crutches.

'That's fine, sir.'

'Everything has been put into operation and it won't be long before the KGB discovers Capuchin's identity. London will not be involved in any way.'

'And our colonial friends, sir?'

'Washington? More confused than ever. They didn't appear to know what to do when the totally unexpected came along. But that will wear off. Sooner or later — perhaps even now — they'll realise they missed something. If Capuchin manages to put two and two together, a friend of mine will be in danger.'

'Yes, sir. What about Rogal?'

'I will leave Mr Rogal to you. He will trap himself.'

The Vicar relaxed a little. It had been a close thing. Capuchin could have found Kocker. Washington could never warn him now, not since they suspected him of working for the Chinese. It was a pity that Capuchin had to be 'caught', but Kocker had to be protected at all costs and, the Vicar had no qualms, the British Ambassador would have been given away as a spy if it meant keeping Kocker's identity secret.

He turned his attention to the latest signal from Kocker. It still puzzled him. Makentov wasn't liked, that was accepted, but his type coming to London was nothing unusual. Most members of the Supreme Soviet had bad reputations, many of them having already visited London over the years, fêted by

Government leaders and trade unionists. Kocker hadn't warned him against any of them.

But he wouldn't rest until the reason for the warning came to him. He locked himself away with up-to-date material on Makentov and studied it, with a giant photograph of the man propped up in front of him as a reminder.

Several times without stopping for a break the Vicar read through the known information on Makentov, but nothing came to the fore. There was not the slightest deviation to suggest he was a threat to Britain's security. Again he read the information, and again, studying in minute detail every photograph available, identifying others in the photographs and tracing their careers; circling within his studying to see if any of the others might be the connection. But, frustratingly, there was still nothing.

He contacted the Director of MI6.

'Vicar here.'

'Yes, sir?' The Director didn't like to hear from the faceless man too often.

'Makentov is to pay a visit shortly. I would like to know why.'

'Who? Makentov? First I've heard of it, sir.'

'Well, he is. Find out about it and call me as soon as you can.'

Nineteen hours later a reply came back. The Vicar had gone three days and two nights without sleep.

'I contacted the Home Office, sir, and they knew nothing about it. Nor did the Foreign Office, nor the Ambassador in Moscow. So far as everyone knew, no approach of any kind had been made by Moscow for a visit to be arranged. They thought I was off my rocker even asking, him being who he is. But since then there's been a development. Quite uncanny. One of our major trade unions has informed the Home Office that it has invited Makentov to be their guest for a week, beginning two weeks from tomorrow. The union involved wasn't very pleased when it learned we already knew he was coming. Apparently it was to be kept secret until the union officials contacted the Home Office. I've had my people inside the union dig a little deeper and it transpires that Makentov himself asked the union to sponsor his visit — to make it appear he was invited.'

'Did he indeed?' The Vicar straightened up. 'What on earth for?'

'That's something we haven't discovered yet, sir.'

'Bring me up to date with the union.'

'One of the largest, sir; strong and militant on the rank-and-file side. The executive committee until recently was controlled by Stalinist-type communists, most of whom were given the chop in the last bout of elections. The majority of the executive was now considered to be moderates, but at least three of them are known by us to be communists. It is a new approach to gaining control of the unions, we believe. Since the introduction of postal ballots the number of communists elected has dropped alarmingly, and a fresh means of infiltration has been put into operation. They purport to be moderate, but when a vital issue comes to the table they suddenly swing their votes. The rank and file see this as a person making the right decision on their behalf.

'It'll take a little time to gather all the information we want, sir, but so far we've managed to discover that two of the executive of the trade union lunched three days ago with a member of the Soviet Embassy. They discussed world trade unions, is what has been said. At the moment it's a guess, but we believe that Makentov's visit was first discussed then. One thing is for sure, sir — the fact that we already knew will have been reported back to Moscow.'

'That is of minor importance. I want to know why he's coming.'

'The official view is that he is part of an exchange scheme. He will spend a week as a guest of the union, visiting a mine, a steelworks, a factory producing plant-hire equipment; and he will sit in on a branch meeting the location of which has still to be decided. In return, the general secretary of the trade union will make a similar visit to Russia in the spring.'

'And unofficially?'

'Nothing, sir. Our people haven't even had a whisper of any kind.'

'Keep digging.'

'Would you like the visit cancelled, sir?'

'What does the Home Office say?'

'They say they can't stop it.'

'Quite right.'

'Is there anything you don't want him to do, sir?'

'No. I don't care a bugger what he does; just so long as I know where he does it and why ... and I want to know beforehand.'

Twenty

Kocker wished he knew more than he did. Contact with the
Vicar was impossible until Grest had finished his investigations.
Grest was searching for him, he knew, and, grudgingly, he
conceded that Grest knew his job. He wasn't quite in the
Vicar's class, but for a man not allowed his own arm he did
well. Too often he was hindered by his superiors – and by the
Supreme Soviet – when they wanted to have a say in what was
to be done. The Chairman demanded and expected, and more
often than not Grest had to oblige. It was a pity, in a way.

Kocker knew that Capuchin and his courier were inactive for
the present, but he didn't know how terrified they were. Grest
had hinted at a Chinese connection but was keeping much to
himself as a precaution. Kocker hoped it was the Vicar's way of
covering for him. He also hoped the Vicar had taken notice of
his warning about Makentov, preferably getting the visit
vetoed. There had been no time to supply more than a name,
for as soon as Grest's discovery was made known, a total ban
was slapped on movements in and out of the country. His own
courier had just got out before the ban was imposed.

It worried Kocker. Grest had found something and it was
political dynamite. How he had missed it was a mystery, but it
had been there in the unexplained files for a number of years. It
could expose him.

Rogal began probing again. After the initial embarrassment of
the affair with Balquidder, he had recovered enough to realise
that something was wrong. Balquidder, and whoever his
controller was, had deliberately held back. They had
deliberately created a lull to gain time; something to cover their

man in the Kremlin. The CIA, he reasoned, had got too close.

Finland was busy. The MANDY and RHODA circuits were brought together and operating along the length of the Finnish/Russian border. They were spread out and to fill the gap the PEANUT AND DOUGHNUT circuits from West Germany and Austria were flown over. Kokkonen and Torne had dropped out of sight and couldn't be located, but he was certain that someone would either try to get in or get out. The European continental doors were closed, with no word crossing in either direction; Prairie Dog would have to have a means of getting out — Finland looked the best bet. Hadn't the new guy, Penton, gone there with some kind of warning? ... That God-damn leaflet. It still hadn't been decyphered. But just let Prairie Dog try, he thought. Just let the bastard try! They would pounce on him like an angry bear.

And there was the dormant CARMELITE circuit. The beggars. The circuit that received no payment of any kind; the circuit that had never been used in its 17 year history. It had been activated just before the doors closed, its task to follow closely the movements of the Supreme Soviet. The CARMELITES, Rogal was certain, Prairie Dog did not know about. They were the ace up the CIA's sleeve. They would find him if the others failed.

Koong contacted Malin again. Malin cringed when he recognised the voice on the other end of the telephone.

'Perhaps we would enjoy a walk ...' was all Koong said.

Malin sat down and wept, shaking from head to foot. The last thing he wanted to do was meet the Oriental, yet he had to. Koong had the ultimate hold. He couldn't get to safety in the West — he would have to comply.

He hadn't washed for days and stubble on his chin was growing into the makings of a beard. His clothes reeked of sweat, drink and tobacco and the only time he ventured out of doors was after dark. There was plenty of drink in his apartment, the only thing he shopped for. Before going out to meet Koong he drank half a litre of Polish Vodka.

His legs had difficulty carrying him. They were like lumps of lead. Although he didn't feel drunk, he felt himself sway from side to side as he walked.

He didn't look round. He knew he wouldn't have to. Koong would be somewhere in the vicinity watching him.

Koong tapped him on the shoulder making him jump with fright.

'Do not look round, Comrade Malin. Please follow the man in front.'

Malin lifted his eyes and saw the huddled figure in front of him. Whoever it was looked no different from the others in the street, hunched in fur coat and hat. He did as Koong ordered and found himself being led into a series of side-streets frequented by alcoholics. For a brief moment it occurred to him that the Chinese knew their way around Moscow better than he did.

They stopped outside a block of three-storey flats, the man in front hiding himself in the shadows.

'Please enter, Comrade,' said Koong. 'Take the second door on your right.'

It was the same as before, Malin found. When he entered the apartment all the lights were out. Koong closed the door behind them and the lights came on. Sitting in the room were two exquisite Chinese girls.

'Please remove your coat, Comrade, and take a seat.'

One of the girls helped him off with his coat, smiling into his face as she did so. The other made him comfortable.

'There are things I must know, Comrade,' Koong said politely. 'I must know why there is so much activity in Moscow just now. Why has travelling been stopped? Why is Major Grest involved in so much internal intrigue? Why is Capuchin afraid? ... Is he in danger of being discovered?'

'It is not Capuchin Major Grest seeks,' Malin said in a low, frightened voice.

'Then who?'

'A British spy, someone higher placed than Capuchin.'

'Ah! Who is this?'

'No one knows.'

'Who told you?'

'I heard it at the Directorate. It's supposed to be secret but most people appear to know.'

'Koong nodded, but not to Malin. It was evident now that Balquidder's meeting with Huan had had an ulterior motive.

'You are unwell, Comrade?' He returned his attention to Malin.

'I need a drink.'

'You have been drinking too much. Like this you will give yourself away.'

'It's only nerves. It'll go away.'

'No more drinking, Comrade.'

Malin nodded. Anything to get back to his apartment.

'You will remain here until you are recovered.'

'What?' Malin began to panic. 'I cannot stay here! I may be wanted at any time by the Directorate.'

'You will be informed if you are required. My people will know.'

Malin rose a little. 'But, I can't!'

'Now, Comrade,' Koong soothed, 'you are in no condition to be at large in Moscow. The KGB would take one look at you and arrest you for being a disgrace to the diplomatic service. It would not be long before they would learn the truth. For your own safety you will remain here. My two colleagues – you may call them Tanya and Natalia – will look after you. One or both of them will be with you at all times. They will provide you with anything you desire, excepting of course alcoholic liquor. They will nurse you through your illness. A few days at the most, then you will be ready to receive the world again ... But a word of warning – do not attempt to leave here until you are ready. Tanya and Natalia are capable of killing you. Afterwards you will be watched to ensure that you do not drink again. You understand?'

Malin's eyes replied that he did. He couldn't move, yet his body was trembling.

Kocker was now in the unique position of having Moscow, Washington and Peking trying to establish his identity.

Twenty-One

'Something else has come up, sir,' the Director of MI6 told the Vicar. 'The Russians have been in contact with the Home Office with the view to a prisoner exchange. They have offered two of our businessmen for George Trayner.'

'Tell me more.'

'The Russian Embassy contacted the Home Office and suggested the exchange; the Home Sec gave the matter consideration, contacted the department Trayner worked for and gave the green light.'

'Why was the go-ahead given?'

'It seems that the information Trayner took to prison with him is now out of date. Moscow can't learn anything from him.'

'Right, fair enough. I want to know the exact date Trayner is to be released and the plans made for him. Most of all I want to know if the plans coincide with Makentov's visit.'

'Trayner is to be released quickly, in two weeks time.'

'Aha! Get me information on Trayner — over the last few months.'

'Yes, sir.'

Twelve hours later the information came.

'Trayner wrote a letter to a friend in London, requesting the friend visit him. This was some months ago. The friend happened to be a member of the Russian trade mission, who was refused permission to visit Trayner. But I am told by the Home Office that a member of the Russian Embassy has been to visit Trayner on four consecutive days. They apparently spoke to great length.'

'Has the Home Office had Trayner under observation?'

'Each of the visits were recorded on film.'

'I should like to see them. I will supply you with an address. I want the films and equipment installed there for my use.'

'Yes, sir.'

A projector was set up in a small warehouse near Southend-on-Sea, used on occasions by Balquidder's department when a safe house outside London was required. It had several entrances to discourage anyone watching comings and goings, one of which was adjacent to the platform at Prittlewell Station, which the Vicar used.

There were three sealed film cans, dated and marked with duration. The Vicar began with the date on which the embassy official arrived. It was too coincidental. Trayner's information was no good to Moscow yet they were going to great lengths to get him out. The timing was curious. Makentov was coming, again an event quickly brought about. And while there was a clampdown on travelling between East and West. Normally, in the case where the information would be useless, the spy would be left to serve his term. He would be looked after when he eventually did get out, but they wanted Trayner out ... which meant there was something he could tell them.

The film showed the Russian, one Nikitai Abramov, arriving at the entrance to the prison, following him through to the VIP visitor's block. He spoke to no one nor touched anything, but just nodded politely to the prison staff, smiling when it was necessary. He was searched before entering the room where he would meet Trayner, to which he didn't object. All objects were removed from his pockets then handed back to him in a sealed brown envelope.

The next shot, inside the visiting room, showed Ambramov enter and take his seat in front of the glass panel separating him from the inmate's side. On request he laid the brown envelope to one side, but in full view of himself, and waited. Two guards took up positions at the rear of the room behind him, one in each corner like statues, impassive.

Trayner was brought in and the film became split, Trayner in one half and Abramov in the other. Trayner nodded slightly to Abramov and sat down. The two guards who'd escorted him took up positions similar to the others.

'You are well?' Abramov said.

'Quite fit, considering the length of time I've been here.'

'You still exercise?'

'Every day, when I can. I also keep my mind active. I'm in charge of the library and read every newspaper that comes in.'

'You are not depressed any more?'

'I got over my depression ten years ago.'

'That is good. The world has changed, but although you have been kept here you have kept up with it. That is a good thing. You know about the release?'

'I was told yesterday. It could have been a lot sooner.'

Now, thought the Vicar. What did he mean by that remark?

'Have you had regular medical check-ups?'

'Her Majesty's prisons make sure no one becomes ill'

It was all like that; nonsense, except for the single remark. Trayner didn't mention why he'd asked someone to come. The camera angle altered often. Their faces were always in view but sometimes their hands came into focus, or their lips to see if they were moving while the other was speaking. There was nothing suspicious.

Which made the Vicar all the more suspicious. Trayner hadn't called Abramov urgently to discuss his health. He didn't like it and watched the film through a second time.

Again there was nothing. Puzzled, the Vicar fed in the second reel. Again it was Abramov, and again they talked about nothing in particular. The third film was the same; there was nothing to suggest that Trayner wanted to speak of something important.

The Vicar switched off and thought. Kocker had warned him about Makentov; Makentov was due to visit when Trayner was released, both events quickly arranged, and all following an urgent letter from Trayner to a Russian in London. He wanted to tell Abramov 'something'.

But he hadn't. He hadn't asked anything or told Abramov anything. Or, the Vicar mused, that was the way things appeared.

He went back to the start, to the first film he watched and began again, staring intently at Trayner's face. There had to be something he'd missed. For an hour he studied the traitor's face, then his hands; maddeningly there was nothing. Another hour, and another ...

Then it came all of a sudden.

Twenty-Two

It was Trayner's eyes. He had looked at the eyes and seen nothing, but for a reason he couldn't explain they suddenly seemed to speak to him. He studied the eyes closely. Trayner's blinking was erratic, sometimes slow, sometimes fast, sometimes rapid in short bursts.

Trayner was using his eyes to communicate in morse code.

He was fascinated. Trayner would know morse of course; he was a spy; it would be part of his job ...

The film was run back to its introduction, the Vicar cutting out the oral conversation at the flick of a switch.

'Why?' Abramov said.

Trayner's reply was abbreviated, like pidgin English. He told Abramov he knew who was responsible for betraying him.

'How? When?'

Trayner related how he was attending a function at the British Embassy in Moscow. He was the Ambassador's personal secretary then. A new trade deal had been signed between the two countries and a reception was held at the embassy. He knew by sight and name all the English present and some of tlhe Russians, but there were Russians he didn't know. At an appropriate moment he passed on a vital item of information; his contact was assistant to a member of the Supreme Soviet.

'Yes?' Abramov's mouth moved, laughing at something Trayner said.

Trayner had watched his contact pass the information on to a man he didn't know. But he could still remember the man's face. The following day he was recalled to London and arrested immediately on landing.

Abramov asked him to describe the man.

'No.'

'No?'

Trayner blinked that he couldn't say anything. The man was highly placed. If word got back that he knew, he would be killed.

'You're certain?'

Trayner replied without abbreviating.

'I've had fifteen years to think about it, haven't I?'

'Rank?'

'Don't know.'

Trayner could remember the night vividly now that the truth had dawned. There was no one below his contact in rank to whom he could have spoken to about the information passed. But there was one man who could be given the information. Normally Russian diplomats did not congregate with each other. They were under orders always to mix with their counterparts ... except in an emergency.

Abramov knew what he meant. He suggested Trayner describe him so that an investigation should begin right away.

Trayner shook his head, using the movement in time with the oral dialogue. The person could well read the report and take precautions.

Abramov promised that everyone would be watched closely. To which Trayner replied that it was not unknown for a person to be murdered in prison.

Abramov thanked him.

Grest's secret was out. Trayner's unmasking had never been explained and when Trayner suddenly asked for someone to visit him it should have been obvious why. The matter hadn't been taken up, but Grest found it in the unexplained files and began adding up. Only a person highly placed could have got the information from Trayner ... and then told London so quickly. Lesser persons would not have such rapid channels of communications.

It shook the Vicar. Trayner could identify Kocker. That should have been impossible, but it was there.

He hurried from the warehouse to London and called Balquidder.

'Can you get into Moscow, Colin?'

'Still open, sir.'

'Good boy. There is something you must do. Activate some of your people . ....'

It had to be quick. The KGB had a start; already well into the task of having Trayner released and most certainly searching for Kocker. The exposure of Capuchin would have to be hastened.

Twenty-Three

'It doesn't look good, Ray,' Joe Mellini said angrily. 'The President is pushing hard for results. Congress is complaining about the amount of revenue that has suddenly been diverted to finance the Finnish end of the operation. Sooner or later someone will want to know why.'

'I can't put my finger on it, Chief,' said Rogal. 'We followed the English example and did nothing about the Portuguese incident. Transit is stopped across the Curtain and Balquidder's people are still inactive. I don't understand what's going on.'

'Capuchin?'

'We don't know. Jesuit was told to report on him but he can't get out until the crisis is over.'

'Christ! If Capuchin is a Peking commie we'll both be looking for another job.'

'I've activated the Carmelites, chief.'

'You what!' Mellini ejaculated. 'Jesus-mothafuckin'-Christ! We can find this guy without using them!'

'I thought ...'

'You God-damned prick! The Carmelites were only to be used when there was an uprising.'

'They'll find him Chief.'

'Yeah, they'll find him okay; but then they'll be useless to us. We won't be able to use them again. Christ! What've you fuckin'-well gone and done? There's no way we can stop them.'

'I'm sorry, Chief.' Rogal was sheepish. 'I thought if Capuchin found him, and if Capuchin is working for Peking, then Peking would find this guy before we did. I wanted our people to find him.'

141

Mellini relented. That part was true. They couldn't afford to take chances on Capuchin.

'Can we get anyone in?'

'I've a group in readiness in Austria, on the Czech border.'

'Too far. They'd never reach Moscow.'

'Then we can't do anything until they lift the Curtain, Chief.'

'Jesus ...'

Balquidder estimated that it would take three days to contact the Vicar's man. He had no name or description; just instructions and the reliance on one of the department's finest employees to carry it through. Arrangements were hasty and twelve hours after the Vicar's call a Russian plane took off from a small privately owned airfield near Dannemora in Sweden. The plane was old but still serviceable, of a type still used in some of the Russian provincial routes. It climbed high immediately on leaving Dannemora, then when over the Baltic dropped to 550 feet. In the dark it didn't have a single light showing.

Within the hour it reached the Gulf of Finland, where the pilot made a sharp turn to port. The nose of the plane now pointed directly at Leningrad, only 250 miles away. It dropped to 300 feet, invisible on the radar screens along the Russian coast. Some forty miles due south of the Finnish capital the pilot instigated a U-turn to starboard, turning wide to take the plane over the Soviet republic of Estonia, where, behind the radar screen, climbing rapidly, the radio-operator made contact with the Estonian capital's airport.

'Hello, Tallinn!' He used a short-range transmission. 'Flight AR 109 from Leningrad requesting permission to land.

Tallinn acknowledged the signal and asked why the flight was one hour earlier than scheduled.

'Security,' the operator replied. 'Please prepare for a landing and have a fuelling tanker on hand for immediate use. Priority is code-Marsh.'

Code-Marsh stirred the control tower at Tallinn. It was the current code used when important officials of the KGB were travelling the country.

'Permission to land on runway three, AR 109. Any

requests?'

'A car to be waiting, and no onlookers.'

'Will comply,' Tallinn said.

The lights in the plane came on and Christopher Bryant sighed with relief. It was an entrance he hadn't attempted before – one that couldn't be used again – but if it came off it would be a coup even the Russians would be forced to admire.

The plane landed without a hitch away from the control tower, where a team of men rushed out to couple-up a fuel tanker. Bryant, alias Leon Alexandrovic, stepped down the ramp, entered the waiting car and drove off. He left the airport by a side gate, acknowledging the salute of the armed guard who closed the gate behind him, then sped away in the direction of Tallinn. He drove for only a few minutes and slowed. The airport's main entrance was just ahead, with large arrows pointing to a two-storey car-park. Apart from a few cars identical to his own the car-park was empty.

It was a short walk to the booking hall and while he waited he heard the plane take off. Given fifteen minutes of uninterrupted flying it would be safe.

He completed the forms handed to him exactly as the airport officials wanted: reasons for travelling; how far; address at destination, etc. His identity papers described him as a security officer attached to the North Atlantic fishing fleet. Tallinn was a base for the vast fishing fleets of Russia and travellers inland were many.

When flight AR 109 called in for landing instructions chaos ensued. The airport was sealed, hordes of grim men in a procession of identical black cars arrived from Tallinn, the nearby air-base was contacted and jet-fighters took to the skies to search for the intruder. The scheduled flight to Leningrad was delayed for two hours; nothing was explained to the frustrated passengers but each one was questioned and their luggage searched before they were allowed to board.

Less than an hour after leaving Tallinn, Bryant landed at Pushkin airport, Leningrad's new artery, and although it was in the early hours of the morning it was a hive of activity. Police were everywhere, everyone was having their papers checked. Bryant had his checked twice before being allowed through to the reception hall. Even there he was under the eye of watching KGB agents. Anyone arriving from Tallinn was suspect. He could imagine that Tallinn itself would be sealed up tighter than a ball-float.

Bryant behaved like an innocent returning from a journey. He bought a newspaper and strolled into the large eating hall for breakfast. A loudspeaker played morning music from the state radio and when the news was read on the hour there was no mention of the mysterious aircraft landing at Tallinn. Not that Bryant expected there to be.

He read the paper through, not because it held any interest for him but because Leningrad was a reader's city. Everyone avidly read newspapers. After an hour he left on a bus for the city centre. The time difference put him an hour ahead of Sweden; while Sweden would be preparing to rise for its daily toil, Leningrad was already on its way.

Bryant made his way to the People's Hall of Literature, once a Royal Palace and now echoing to the footsteps of a million schoolchildren each year. It was a vast complex, open twenty-four hours a day. It had its own security department, cafeterias and an independent power supply. It also had many toilets and it didn't take Bryant long to change from a dark-blue suit to a brown and become Ivan Simovic. Leon Alexandrovic no longer existed, as had already been established elsewhere. Speedy communications with Moscow confirmed there were a number of Alexandrovics in the fishing fleets, but none with the Christian name of Leon. Nor did anyone by the name of Leon Alexandrovic have permission to travel.

When Bryant, with a pair of black-rimmed glasses across his eyes, boarded the jet destined for Moscow under his new name, Leningrad's KGB were combing the city looking for him under his previous description. Grest was informed. Bryant's description was telegraphed to him, advising him that an English or American spy was on his way to Moscow to contact a traitor. Grest arrived at Moscow's domestic airport while the plane was half-way between the two cities.

When Bryant stepped down from the plane at Moscow airport he was prepared for a check of some kind, even the most stringent of checks. Armed men, civilian and military,

144

formed a guard across the tarmac, stopping each person leaving the plane. Couples and families were split up, taken into rooms out of sight of other airport users, questioned, then either reappearing or simply disappearing. But Bryant reasoned that the KGB couldn't be certain he was on the flight. There were other ways of reaching Moscow from Leningrad. He was asked many questions, his papers were checked and re-checked, but no one bothered to call the Institute of Physical Health in Leningrad to check on his claim of being the sub-director. He was allowed through.

On leaving the airport he didn't waste time, but he did not hurry. With the purpose of an official of his rank he hailed a taxi-driver and grunted an address in the south-east of the city. The journey took an hour. He paid off the driver and went into a large store. Again, in a toilet, he changed, this time throwing away the brown jacket and donning a thin windcheater hidden in the attaché-case. In the store he bought a fur-lined jacket and cap, and with his glasses in his pocket he once again became another person.

As Andrei Lobnor, Bryant used public transport to take him to the west of the city where, immediately on identifying himself with a code-word, he was installed in a worker's tenement apartment used as a safe house. His contact was an elderly man, a foreman in a factory making electrical wall sockets. He left Bryant to stay with his daughter.

Bryant rested. There would be a hue and cry for him before long and it would not be good for him to be seen. He could not use the lights of the apartment, nor watch TV; until he departed he had to content himself with padding around the flat and listening to the radio with its volume turned low.

Grest followed Bryant's trail, always a step behind. When Bryant was safely hidden in the apartment the trail ended at the department store. A counter assistant remembered the man who bought a hat and coat, describing him fairly accurately, but where he had gone afterwards was not known. Grest was pleased though. All he had to do was to have his suspects watched; sooner or later one of them would be contacted. Everything was turning out fine.

He also received a cable from London telling him that Colin

Balquidder was to attend a function organised by the Chinese Trade Mission, to celebrate the massive deal struck between London and Peking. An invitation had been obtained for him, if he still had business in London.

Twenty-Four

Within twenty-four hours Grest was one of the many guests at a London guild hall where the celebrations were taking place. Balquidder was there, much the centre of attraction. He limped slightly but looked remarkably fit following his ordeal at the hands of his American colleagues. The Americans were there, watching everyone, and wondering what Grest was doing there while the shutters were down.

Grest didn't accost Balquidder. Everyone who was anyone in politics or business were surrounding him, heaping him with praise. When that died down he would make his move.

Grest invited tenders. Balquidder was, so far as everyone was concerned, an employee of the Department of Trade and Industry: Grest played the part of his Russian equivalent. Russia wanted a new computerised system for storing the next census intended for the mid-eighties. Offers came in his direction and, as was expected of him, he politely received them all, promising they would be given consideration. It gave him the contact he needed to talk with Balquidder. They played the usual game first.

'Mr Balquidder?'

'In person.' Balquidder beamed.

'My name is Grest; Zibor Grest; employed by the Soviet Trade Ministry.'

'Welcome to London, Mr Grest.'

'Thank you; and from what I hear, you are to be congratulated.'

'This? ... Oh, I just happened to be in the right place at the right time.'

'Nonetheless, it was a magnificent achievement; particularly when the order was all but destined for America.'

'Ah, well. These things happen … I believe your government is interested in some equipment?'

'Yes.'

'Then, my dear chap. This is the place to be. Just tell me your wont and I'll introduce you to the appropriate people.'

'I was thinking of approaching you, Mr Balquidder.'

'We would certainly appreciate any business from your government.'

'I see some Americans,' said Grest. 'One of them appears troubled.'

Rogal did appear troubled. He was even more troubled since Grest and Balquidder sat down together.

'Yes,' Balquidder drawled. 'Poor chap has something on his mind, I believe.'

'I wonder why?' Grest gave Balquidder a sly look.

'I should imagine the reason will come to you in due course.' Balquidder replied. 'Something to do with Peking, I hear.'

'You have a lively city, Mr Balquidder.' Grest changed the subject. He had been given a signal by the Englishman.

'Your first visit?'

'No, I have been here on occasions in the past.'

That much is honest, thought Balquidder.

'Yes …' Balquidder sighed with satisfaction. 'London has always had an attraction. Much as many other cities have …'

Grest reacted on cue. 'You have visited Moscow, Mr Balquidder?'

'Haven't had the pleasure, old chap.'

'Moscow holds many wonders.'

'So I believe.'

'You have friends there?'

'I know people who have been to Moscow.'

'I would be interested to learn their reactions to our city.'

'Oh, I don't think I can remember everything they told me.'

'Your friends would be English, of course? They would see Moscow differently from an American, for example, or a German.'

'I have friends in different parts of the world. Many of them have visited Moscow.'

'We too are cosmopolitan. Probably more nationalities live in Moscow than live in London.'

'Good grief, yes, old chap. I have friends who speak of aquaintances in Moscow who turn out to be of Chinese origin. Yet they speak of them as I would a chap from Sussex.'

'Yes, many of our people are Chinese.'

'Odd people, in a way ...' Balquidder seemed to delve into his memory. 'They are Chinese, yet they consider themselves to be Russian.'

'As it should be,' said Grest.

'And conversely there are the people who in features are obviously European Russians, yet seemingly claim homage with China.'

'Yes, more is the pity.' Grest got the point.

'Everyone has this kind of anomaly, unfortunately.'

'It is rare in Russia.'

'Quite ...' Balquidder eased himself in his chair and smiled a happy smile, as if recalling a pleasant memory. 'I remember chatting to one of your chappies some years back. Can't really find his name in the old brainbox, but I believe it was when our two governments had talks about exchanging two fellows who'd been naughty ... our chap's name was Sinclair, I think. Yes, we were of the same opinion regarding the Chinese. Didn't trust them an inch, old chap, neither of us; but we couldn't help agree that the Great Wall was something for the entire world to be proud of, and not just the Chinese. We spoke for hours just about the Great Wall ...'

'A remarkable achievement for a backward race at the time.'

'... Can't quite remember his name ...'

'Perhaps you will visit my country one day, Mr Balquidder? We have so much more to offer than China.'

Balquidder pursed his lips. 'Don't doubt it for a second, old chap! Bags of romantic history attached to Russia, you know.'

'We are proud of her.'

'Jolly well proud, too. First class.'

'It has been an enjoyable evening, Mr Balquidder.'

'You're leaving, old chap?'

'I must, I'm afraid. I waited until most of the euphoria died down before I made my government's intentions known. It was so busy at the beginning.'

'Please to have had your company, old chap. Jolly good show!'

Grest excused himself. Balquidder had given him two items of information. Rogal was worried about the Chinese, the reason for which would become apparent, according to Balquidder. The second item was most interesting. Balquidder openly gave him the leader of a Chinese spy-ring operating in Moscow. It was only a matter of looking back in records to see who conversed with the Englishman at the time of the exchange.

But Balquidder hadn't been so clever. He hadn't mentioned anything about his own spy-ring — nor had Grest expected him to — but why was he giving away the Chinese?

That was simple enough. Balquidder was worried. He was giving away the Chinese to take the heat off his own people. That meant he was closer to the English spy than he had imagined.

And Rogal? Balquidder hinted that the reason would come. Why should Rogal be worried about the Chinese? Had Peking penetrated Washington's spy-ring? Time would tell … In a short time he would round up all three spy rings. Peking! London ! Washington! … All of them.

Balquidder telephoned the Vicar and reported that another small item had been taken care of.

Bryant made his move as Grest returned to Moscow. His briefing had been detailed and explicit. He knew exactly where in the appropriate government building the contact could be found. Using the last of his 'credentials' he joined the queue at a Metro station close to the safe house, cursing with the other passengers at the cruel weather.

Bryant was a handsome man. Nearly thirty, he had been in and out of Russia illegally several times in the past, and always his youngish, smooth, happy face had been a boon. His blue eyes attracted both men and women; he could speak with a Moscow accent and his normal smart walk gave him an aura of importance. People who noticed him remembered him; never in a suspicious manner, but as a tribute to Russian manhood.

He knew now, though, that things were different. In the past the KGB were never aware of his presence, but in the last two days the entire Russian security system would have a description of him. He would be remembered all the way from Tallinn.

That he would never be able to work in Russia again didn't worry him. Russian assignments always made him apprehensive; although he always managed to keep out of the way of the KGB the time would come when they would take two steps instead of one.

The assignment he had now was simple enough. All he had to do was contact 'K', give him his instructions, then wander into the embassy for a trip home under the diplomatic cloak.

He missed Grest by seconds. When he reached the building where the contact had his office, a guard stopped him while his papers were checked, his photograph and fingerprints taken. The papers were handed back to him and as he swivelled round to put them into his inside pocket Grest crossed the entrance inside the building.

Bryant whistled softly as he strode along the main corridor; he didn't notice Grest's back as the other disappeared along the side corridor. He mounted a staircase as if he did the same journey every day. Two flights later he stopped at a notice board. It was exactly as London had described. It was, he had been told, an attempt by the KGB to give the department a 'family' feeling.

The board was covered with personal messages; men and women inviting friends to meet them at various locations within the vast building, or in restaurants or cafés outside. Bryant pinned his notice to the board, standing for some time reading the others and joined in a short conversation with a young girl who displayed some concern over the absence of a note from a boyfriend.

Twenty-Five

Grest was tired but something unexpected had arisen when he landed in Moscow. He was immediately taken to the Directorate and given a report to read. A frightened, near-tearful diplomatic courier was seated in an empty office flanked by two guards. He nearly fainted with terror when Grest began questioning him.

'Tell me in your own words what happened, Comrade.'

'I had just returned from Oslo, having a drink in the cultural palace ... An Oriental ... I never saw him before ... stopped beside me and smiled ... I felt his hand go into my pocket ... I was scared ... I finished my drink and left ... And when I felt in my pocket I found the note.'

Grest picked up the piece of paper and showed it to the courier.

'Is this it?'

The courier read it: WE MUST MEET. 'Yes, Comrade Major.'

'Then what happened?'

'I rushed home ... away from him ... and the same night someone telephoned me ... asking me to go out for our usual walk.'

'Did you go out for a walk?'

'No!' The courier shook his head rapidly.

'Why didn't you report this sooner?'

'I was afraid, Comrade Major.'

'Of what?'

'Of being arrested.'

'For what?'

'Treason.'

'You are not a traitor, Comrade, are you?'

'No, Comrade Major.'

'What made you report the incident?'

'I was afraid.'

'What of, this time?'

'I don't know, Comrade Major. I was afraid to report it and afraid not to.'

'It is a serious matter, Comrade, not to report an incident that is harmful to the people of Russia.'

'I ... I ...'

'However, it is up to your superiors what is to be done with you. In the meantime, you will deposit your credentials with me, and until your superiors take up the matter you will spend some time at the de-briefing centre at Kazator.'

'But, Comrade—'

The courier made to protest but the guards by his side were already in action. He was roughly handled; in seconds all his pockets were emptied, the contents thrown on the floor, then held by both arms he was escorted away. He whimpered as the guards took him. He knew all about Kazator, the KGB village on the eastern outskirts where people were sent.

Grest glowed with pride. The spy-rings were beginning to crumble. The English and Americans were worried, and the Chinese were trying to recruit. But did the Chinese know Balquidder had given them away?

He collected the contents of the courier's pockets, hurried them along to a laboratory where they would be analysed for Oriental traces, then ran up the stairs to the second floor to report to the Supreme Soviet. On the way he cast a quick eye over the notice board. There was no message from his brother telling him to phone his mother, as there normally was once every week. He hurried on.

Kocker passed the same notice board seconds later, paused and went on. Then he stopped in his tracks and walked back. The notice that caught his eye was something he hadn't expected to see. K, MUST SEE YOU, V.

A swift look round told him that the corridor was empty and in a single sweep the notice was off the board and in his pocket. Fifty-five seconds later it was torn to shreds and flushed down a toilet.

'There is,' said Grest, when the Supreme Soviet was assembled, 'a trio of spy-rings operating at this moment in Moscow. All Russia's enemies are here stealing our secrets – Peking, London and Washington.'

The reaction was predictable. The existence of English and American spies was suspected, but Chinese spies was something new. The Soviet cursed and swore; they screeched for someone to be brought before a court, half accusing each other of having caused the situation.

The Chairman was beside himself with fear and anger.

'We have been too easy with our enemies,' he ranted. 'By trying to be friendly with them, this is what happens. They come ... they steal our secrets ... they turn our people into traitors ... It was a mistake. We should be sealed off from the West!'

'They must be caught.' Comrade Brugi quoted the obvious. 'Immediately.'

'Soon, comrade,' soothed Grest. 'It will not be long. I am gradually getting closer to them.'

'We need progress.'

'The Englishman, Balquidder, told me something that I am about to act on. It will allow me to penetrate the Peking spy-ring. From there I will break it entirely. The English spy we can count on being identified within the next two weeks – perhaps even less. Comrade Makentov will visit England and escort our comrade when he is released. The American spy-ring is a little more difficult to identify, but I have a lead which I would rather not disclose at present.'

The Chairman grunted. He was far from satisfied but there was nothing he could do otherwise. Had he known that Grest was lying as far as the American spy-ring was concerned, he would have gone berserk. Grest was as close to netting the American spy-ring as the Pope was to turning communist.

Grest went on. 'The American, Rift, told us that the leader of the English spy-ring takes his orders from a man in London with the code-letter of "V". He could tell us ...'

Suddenly he stopped. The Soviet stared at him, puzzled. He had gone pale.

Grest ran from the conference centre. In the corridor he threw people to one side in his haste to reach the notice board. When he reached it he cried out with despair.

He ran back to the Soviet, shouting and screaming for guards; inside the conference centre he pressed a button that activated a general alarm. Armed guards appeared from nowhere and all outside doors were sealed. Office doors became locked electronically and supervisors began a roll-call. Heads were counted and telephones rang while the whereabouts of persons missing from their offices were traced.

Breathlessly Grest explained to the Soviet the message he'd noticed on the board prior to entering the centre. Now it was gone.

'Here!' The Chairman trembled like a jelly. He behaved as if someone had just declared a nuclear war. 'In this building!'

Grest was also shaking. The incident illustrated just how deep the English spy had been planted.

'That's it!' The Chairman threw his hands in the air. 'Our frontiers must. be closed immediately. No movement whatsoever. Not even embassy staff on diplomatic service ...' He halted to let his words get their meaning across. It was a measure Moscow had never taken before. No government had taken the step during all the years of diplomatic traffic. There would be howls of protest, but Moscow had to protect herself. '... Not until they are caught will our frontiers be open again.'

An instant inquiry began. Teams of KGB interrogators flooded the building and every man and woman were questioned. For the Supreme Soviet the interrogation was cursory, but the farther down the line the interrogators went, the more intensified their questions.

Bryant was long gone. He had been in the building less than ten minutes. By the time Grest pressed the panic button he was resting in the safe house.

Kocker was disturbed. He had so many years before had the Vicar's word that their only contact would be through a Polish diplomat; it was always a one-way traffic and the message on the notice board was a shock. It had to be for him, for passing the board every day taught him that no one called 'V' ever asked to speak to anyone called 'K'. It should not have been done, but he knew that the Vicar had somehow discovered why Makentov was to visit London. The contact would have instructions for him. They were really unnecessary, but he would have to meet the contact just the same.

Twenty-Six

Nikolai Malin was fully recovered from his drinking bout. The girls had looked after him as Koong promised. Most of the time he'd been naked. The girls had taught him things he'd never dreamed of and when it was time to go he felt a little reluctant.

'Comrade Malin,' Koong clapped his hands with glee. 'How well you look. If you could have seen yourself when you came here. You were a shameful sight to behold.'

Malin smiled. 'I feel wonderful.'

'Good, good. Now you can rejoin the world. It is time that people saw you. In Moscow one can be missed. In your position it would be better if you at least report to your superior.'

'If you think that would be best.'

'I do, Comrade. And to help you enjoy your extended leave I have brought you a little money.'

'No!' Malin gasped when he saw the pile of American dollars. 'It is too much money to have in Moscow.'

'Spend it slowly, Comrade. There is much one can do with dollars in Moscow.'

That was true. People would do anything to get hold of dollars or pounds or marks; they opened many doors. But to have too much was to invite trouble.

'If it became known that I had so much money there would be an inquiry. I never know if the KGB have searched my apartment. They do, you know.'

'Then there is something you can do with it.'

Malin stared into the odd face and waited for the solution.

'You can use it to recruit others to work for you.'

Malin was aghast. This was something he hadn't expected. 'I

can't! I wouldn't know how.' He protested.

'It is much easier than you think, Comrade. People say things you do not notice, but when you listen for them you spot them easily. You will know what to do when the time comes. You could begin by selling some of your money to someone whom you know is easily led.'

Malin stood with his mouth open. He was becoming deeper and deeper involved. But he had no option.

'It's risky.'

'Of course, but with careful selection you will get away with it.'

'I don't know.'

'Get dressed now, Comrade, and return to your normal life. Everything will turn out well.'

It was late afternoon when he reached the Directorate, still time to speak to his superior, then he would return to his own apartment and make plans for when he got to the West. That's where he was going just as soon as travel was allowed again. The Chinese could whistle for their spies.

There was some activity when he reached the Directorate but no one was inclined to say what was going on. He was still reasonably calm when he asked his superior if there was something for him to do.

'Not at present, Nikolai.' The other's face was grim. 'Everything is at a standstill ... haven't you heard?'

'Heard what, Comrade? I've been relaxing since I saw you last. I put work right out of my mind.'

'Things are serious, Nikolai. Everyone is being watched. There are spies at large close to the Supreme Soviet. Only a few hours ago one of them had the audacity to communicate with his contact – inside this very building. The KGB are going mad.'

Malin's mouth dried up.

'And they say that the arrest of a Chinese spy-ring is imminent.'

Malin froze.

'It would be better if you went home again, Nikolai. Here you will be stopped and questioned; you with regular visits to the West, they will want to know about any small relationships you might have had with women there. You know what they can make out of that.'

'Yes,' Malin's voice croaked. 'I'll do as you suggest, Comrade.'

'I'll call you when you're required.'

Malin panicked. He tried hard to remain calm while he negotiated the stairs to the street, but his heart was beating like a mongol drum. When he did reach the street it took all his self control to stop from being sick. He walked fast, away from the entrance and turned a corner, then ran. He ran hard, fast, looking neither right nor left, not stopping until he reached the entrance to the Metro.

The train couldn't come quick enough, nor did it travel fast enough when it did pick up its passengers. He was aware that many people were looking at him in his distressed state. Someone would become suspicious, but he didn't care; he would get his money and escape.

At his apartment he tore the cap from a bottle of English gin, swallowing some of the clear liquid, then leaned against a wall while his body racked itself with coughing. The money was still there. The KGB hadn't done a spot check on his apartment. That was something to be thankful for.

He couldn't contain himself. He drank some more, bundled a few articles of clothing into a bag and had a last look round. There was nothing else he could take, not even if he wanted to. He would go and see Tanya and Natalia. They would hide him until he could get out.

Kocker left his office at eight in the evening. The questioning had dropped off and only a handful were still being held. A few had been taken away but most had been allowed to leave.

There was a good layer of snow in the street and it was bitter cold. The Siberian winds were finding their way through the streets. It would be an even colder winter than usual, throughout which there would be dreadful goings-on within the government. For a moment he wondered how many people in the streets knew what was going on. Very few. But then it didn't do them any good to know what went on.

He saw the man waiting for him. It was only for a fraction of a second while the man was making sure he was who he was.

But a fraction of a second was all he required. He had spent too many nights in the ruins of Berlin, where nights had never been darker, to miss someone in a brightly lit street, even though the other was in shadow.

It wouldn't be the KGB, he reasoned. They would not have him followed. Nor would it be the Vicar, for the contact was waiting for him at the safe house. Nor could it be the Chinese because they did not know he existed. Neither could it be the Americans. Yet it had to be one of them.

How? Why? Why should someone think he should be followed?

His car was close-by and he climbed in. It took a minute or two to clear the windscreen and rear-window of snow, but the engine kicked over straight away. There was a familiar crunch of snow coming from the tyres when he pulled away, and glancing in his rear-view mirror he saw another car pull out behind him. Whoever it was had an influential position of some kind.

Kocker drove leisurely without looking back. He drove to the four points of the compass on the city's outskirts, then back to the centre for a snack in one of the special shops. It gratified him to know that the man was still following him. He came into the shop. Without appearing to, Kocker studied him.

He searched his brain to put a name to the face. He recognised the man but for the moment his name escaped him.

On his second cup of coffee it came to him. The man was Josef Kalinan, head of the news section of the country's internal radio-broadcasting network. At least once every week Kalinan sent drafts of news broadcasts to the Supreme Soviet for vetting before they were relayed over the air. He ranked high in the party but was only a co-opted member of the KGB, an honorary member, for his position held no real standing within the espionage departments.

Which then posed a problem. Kalinan was not employed by the KGB, therefore would not be following him in that respect. The KGB controlled all other policing and law-enforcing departments, so that counted him out as working in any way for the government.

With applied logic he rose with the answer. When

Washington first discovered there had to be an English spy in the Kremlin, she would have issued orders that he was to be identified as quickly as possible. The only method she could use would be to have every high-ranking official followed until one made a move. It could be no other way. And that meant there had to be another American ring he didn't know about.

Well, Kalinan, thought Kocker, your controller will rue the day he set you on me.

Kocker had a wisp of a smile on his face when he left the special shop. He took his time, giving Kalinan time to catch up. They reached their cars together.

Satisfied that no one else was on his trail Kocker drove to within a hundred metres of the safe house. Although he'd arranged the house some years before it was the first time he'd paid a visit. He'd created the network that was run from it, but none of the network knew he existed.

He made sure there were no other vehicles in the vicinity when he left his car, except Kalinan. He doused his lights, stuck a KGB permit below the windscreen and slid into the cold night. Above him the apartment was in darkness.

He tapped lightly on the door, 'K' in morse. Nothing happened and he tapped again, the second time adding 'V'. Some seconds passed and he detected a shuffling from inside.

The door opened a fraction and part of a face peered at him; below the face was the snout of a silenced Luger.

'I have an appointment with the Vicar,' Kocker said quietly.

The door opened wider to allow him entry, but the Luger never wavered. Kocker closed the door behind himself, walked towards the small sitting-room with his arms raised; light coming through the window from the street enabled him to find a chair.

'You might as well put the gun away, my friend,' he said. 'Nothing can be said until you do.'

Bryant found a chair and lowered the gun.

'Does it surprise you to see me?' Kocker smiled.

'I couldn't give a bugger who you are, old mate,' said Bryant. 'I just do my job.'

'You have led Major Grest a merry dance.'

Bryant shrugged. 'I've had to do it before, and I suppose I'll do it again.'

'You know that all travel is banned?'

'I'll get out.'

'The embassy is being watched more closely than usual, my friend. It would pay you well to stay clear of it for a time. Your description is known.'

'I'll risk it.'

'All right, my friend. You look after yourself … Now, tell me what you were sent for.'

'You have to protect yourself. London has gone to great lengths to cover for you, but now you must also do something.'

'I have already taken some precautions.'

'There are others you must take …'

Kocker listened and smiled. The Vicar was perceptive. They had both thought of the same thing, but to ensure complete success the Vicar had made an addition.

'You may report that I will do everything suggested, my friend.'

'Good,' said Bryant. Now I can leave. You don't know what it's like stuck in a place like this for hours on end.'

'But, I do, my friend … Oh, I do.'

'You weren't followed, I take it?'

Kocker smiled.

Bryant acknowledged the smile. It was a foolish question to ask. 'The sooner you leave the sooner I can get to the embassy. They will change my appearance. I can go home then.'

'Yes,' Kocker sighed. 'Home. Who can call what country home?' He rose, straightening his coat. 'This is my home, and yet it is not.'

Bryant shrugged. He was indifferent to Kocker's thoughts on patriotism.

At the door to the sitting-room Kocker stopped. 'Be careful, my friend. There are many people you should not trust.'

'I'll look after myself … cheers.'

Kocker half-turned. Bryant couldn't see the muzzle of the silencer poking through the folds of Kocker's coat. It spat fire, the bullet tearing through Bryant's heart.

Kocker moved fast then. He didn't touch the body but went back into the sitting-room and carried out a carefully designed

162

plan; this was something he and the Vicar had agreed on. By the side of the radio-set was a hand-written list of radio frequencies for Russian regional transmissions, a normal item in a Russian household. Kocker added five more frequencies, each one used by the BBC overseas service for transmissions in French. That complete he padded into the small kitchen, looking around until he found a cookery book. Every second page of the book contained photographs of dishes that could easily be concocted by the average Russian housewife. He did what was necessary with the cookery book then went back to the bedroom and felt underneath the crudely made wardrobe. The bottom served his purpose admirably. Next was the bathroom; underneath the toilet basin rim he felt for space.

When it was complete he left. He hadn't made a sound, nor left any prints behind.

Kalinan was still there, perhaps fifty metres behind his own car which was covered with snow. The man was foolish. His car was also covered with snow, but he had kept his windscreen wipers going and the clear glass made him stick out like a sore thumb.

Kocker by-passed his own car for Kalinan's. A dark shadow moved quickly behind the clear screen, the red glow of a cigarette end shot across the screen as Kalinan's hand moved, like a shooting star in the sky.

He opened the off-side, rear passenger door and climbed in, met a smell of stale sweat, cigarette smoke and a sickly warmth. Kalinan's eyes became large and round.

'Good evening, Comrade Kalinan, of the State Commission for Broadcasting. What important news item brings you to this district?'

Kalinan stammered. 'I came to visit a friend.'

'And does your friend live in several districts at once, Comrade?'

Kalinan started. He was caught. How could he explain away trailing a member of the Supreme Soviet? There was a small hand-gun taped below the dashboard that would be his only way out.

Kocker was quicker. A bullet smashed Kalinan's hand into the steering column. Another followed, this time entering

Kalinan's groin. An artery split and blood spewed from the wound.

'You will have to be quick, Comrade Kalinan, if you wish to survive,' said Kocker matter-of-factly. Let's say you attempted to stop a foreign spy running away from a crime and you were shot for your troubles. You will become a hero. I have a radio in my car and can have an ambulance here in three minutes. If this is the course you wish to take, tell me everything I wish to know. If it is not, then die.'

Kalinan was listening; at the same time moaning and trying to staunch the flow of blood from his leg..

'What?' he gasped.

'Who do you work for?'

'America.'

'What is your group called?'

'We are known as the Carmelites.'

'Sleepers?'

'Yes.'

'Who is your controller?'

'I receive my instructions from a colleague with the commission. His name is Peter Nevsky.'

'You're a liar!' Kocker snapped.

'No, no!' Kalinan wailed. 'It's the truth!'

'Keep talking.'

'Nevsky knows how many are in the group. We were activated by the Voice of America, with instructions to follow the high-rankers.'

'Why?'

'It is suspected there is an English spy somewhere in the Soviet. We were to find out who, approach and compromise him, force him to work for the Americans. The English don't know about us.'

'Now you know.'

Kalinan nodded.

'Take out a piece of paper and a pen.'

Kalinan stumbled with his good hand and managed to take both from a pocket.

'Write the name of your controller on the paper ... and the words "report to" underneath.'

Kalinan did as he was told.

'Put it under your seat.'

Kalinan leaned forward and pushed the paper under his seat. His neck was bare. Kocker pressed the muzzle of his silencer against it. Kalinan died with his head mixed in the remains of the steering wheel.

Kocker nodded with satisfaction. He leaned over the front seat, switched off the windscreen wipers and dropped the gun on the front passenger seat. Grest, he reasoned, would decide that Kalinan had been killed with his own gun. From a pocket he pulled out two $100 bills, stuffed them into one of Kalinan's pockets, then feeling his clothes to make certain he had no blood on him, stepped out of the car to rejoin his own. Kalinan's windscreen was already snowing over and it would be some days before anyone took any notice of it. It would just be a car snowed in. Within an hour there would be nothing to suggest that anyone had been near it.

Twenty-Seven

Malin rapped on the door of the apartment used by Koong and his two girls. His heart was pounding and every few seconds he looked behind in fear. No one replied to his knocks. He became desperate. He banged and kicked, shouting for Tanya and Natalia to let him in, but no sound came from inside. A door opened close by and a man appeared shouting at him. If he didn't keep his voice down the police would be called. Did he want to spend two years in prison for being a public nuisance?

Malin took to his heels. He couldn't use taxis since all drivers were duty-bound to check the identity of their passengers. Arriving at a bus-stop he waited impatiently for one to come; none did so he ran again, running until he reached the Metro. He had to find a place to hide until he could get out.

Desperately he tried to remember the address of a girl he used to go around with. It was two years since he'd seen her last. He'd been in love with her, prepared to marry her, until he discovered she'd several men friends. For 'favours' she'd been going to bed with men who could use the special shops.

He wished he could remember the last address she'd given him; it was somewhere in the south of the city. She might help him out if he could find her.

While the train raced through the tunnels the name of the street came back, but not the number; he was going in the right direction.

At his destination he ran once more, and not knowing where she lived he chose an apartment and knocked. A tired housewife answered his knock and demanded to know what he wanted.

'I'm looking for Lena Molodechno,' he said. 'She lives in this street but I don't know the number.'

'She doesn't live here!' The woman said and slammed the door.

He tried several apartments; no one knew of her. It worried him even more. He was showing his face. Then came some luck. He knocked on the door where Lena had once lived; the address she'd moved to when they broke up.

'That slut!' A woman said over her husband's shoulder. 'She was thrown out of here ages ago.'

'Where can I find her, please?'

'Try Voroshilov street, number 25.'

The street wasn't far away, although he knew it as in an area not in keeping with the man's memory. It was run-down, reserved for those out of favour with the party. Again he took to his heels, arriving in Voroshilov Street breathless and anxious. Number 25 wasn't hard to find. It was the tallest apartment block in the street, partly damaged during the war but rebuilt to ease the chronic housing shortage.

Lena looked at him strangely when she replied to his knock.

'Well ...' She tried to appear inviting. 'Look who's here.'

'Can I come in?' Malin was shaking.

'Sure, Nikolai. It's not often old friends come to visit.'

A weight dropped from his shoulders when the door closed behind him. At least he was in shelter.

'It's been a long time, Nikolai.'

She was different. Her clothes were scruffy, her hair unkempt. She needed several good meals. She fitted in with the dingy surroundings.

'Can you put me up for a few days, Lena?'

Lena recognised trouble. 'Go away! We can do without the police here.'

'Only for a few days ... Look, I can pay!' He took out his bundle of dollars and offered Lena fifty.

Fifty dollars could be ten times their worth in roubles. 'You'll need food and drink.' She said. 'That'll cost another fifty.' Malin couldn't argue. He gave it over.

'You wait here, Nikolai.' She got her coat. 'I'm going out to do some shopping.'

Later she tried to pump him for information but he refused to be drawn. Lena, on the other hand, was talkative. With vodka inside her following her biggest meal in days, she was in clover. Malin learned she had contracted a disease from a friend who had just returned from the West. The doctor reported her and she lost her job and fine apartment. Now she worked only when one of the local shops was short of assistants. She was barely surviving. He also learned she was supplementing her income by selling herself to some of the other apartment dwellers.

'I hope the KGB doesn't come knocking, Nikolai.'

'They won't.'

'Would you like to renew our friendship?' She smiled at him.

Malin wouldn't have touched her if she'd paid him.

Twenty-Eight

Before Leonev Chukotev left for his office the next morning he was surprised when he found a small package pushed through his mail-box. This was unusual since all correspondence was normally sent to his office.

The package had a Moscow postmark, posted late the night before, made from a paper not used at the Directorate. At the breakfast table he opened it, half-listening to his wife and youngest son arguing over who should prepare the rubbish to be put down the disposal chute.

Had they not been arguing they might have seen the 500 American dollars, the list of names and radio frequency lists for both the VOA and BBC Russian, German and French broadcasts.

Chukotev quickly shoved the articles back into the package, hurried them through to the small room he used as a study, making sure the door was locked behind him. The dollars were what first took his attention. He counted them twice, his hands shaking; they were crisp and new, in series; they still had a fresh smell.

The frequency lists were unimportant so far as he was concerned. They could be obtained at any time from the Directorate; but the list of names was something he couldn't understand. Why had they been sent to him? Indeed, why the package? Someone had obviously made a mistake.

He couldn't forget there was a rampant spy-fever in progress, and what he had in front of him could undoubtedly be taken as something belonging to a foreign spy, or a spy's controller. The money could be 'traitor's wages'; the frequencies when to listen, and the list of names a spy-ring.

On the other hand it could be a KGB plant. He could be being put to a test. The KGB did that at times.

What to do? He could walk straight into Directorate security with the package and explain. If it was a KGB plant everything would be all right. But what if it wasn't? What if it was intended for a foreign spy? In that case it wasn't the ideal time to approach the KGB, not with the eruptions going on – for didn't they suspect someone in the Directorate? Anyone in possession of anything considered suspicious was automatically investigated.

It would be better, he decided, to just say nothing and wait until everything blew over. The money could never be traced, nor would anyone admit to having sent it to him. He locked it away in his desk, knowing that his wife and son would never dream of trying to get inside.

There was another surprise in store for him when he reached the office. Lying in his 'in-tray' was an envelope similar to the one he'd received earlier at home. It bore no postmark or stamp, had been delivered by internal mail, posted inside the Directorate. There was nothing to indicate where it came from. Beginning to get worried he shoved it into his inside pocket.

Capuchin was working normally. He was completely unaware that Malin had panicked and ran, but he too was afraid. He also intended to depart Moscow as soon as the ban on travelling was lifted. The Chinese approaching him had destroyed his cover; if they find him so could the KGB. They had given him some money he couldn't use – not in Moscow, but it would be helpful when he escaped to the West. And there would be plenty more to come; the Americans would pay well for the information he could give them.

In Paris, Huan; and in London, Balquidder, the Vicar, Rogal and Mellini, all at some time during the day and evening, without realising it, looked to the east wondering how events were progressing. Huan had found some of the people working for the Americans and was looking forward to the time when information would be flowing. Rogal and Mellini were pinning their hopes on the Carmelites, waiting for the ban to lift so that word could come out; waiting to hear from Jesuit — if Capuchin was working for Peking. They were also waiting for Balquidder's department to make a move. But no one was stirring. Balquidder's people had gone to ground.

Balquidder and the Vicar wondered if Kocker was handling his end satisfactorily — Kocker couldn't be allowed to go down. But whatever all three powers thought and wondered, there was nothing they could do but wait. No one moved.

Grest received an internal memo informing him that a second courier had come forward with an unusual communication. There appeared to be a Chinese involvement.

He also found some information he had been searching for.

Chukotev went straight to his study when he returned home in the evening. Trembling, he opened the package from work. Inside was another pile of dollars, another 500; another list of names — identical to the one in the morning post, but alongside the names were code-names. A second sheet of paper had addresses on it, locations dotted around the city; another with locations of public parks and libraries. A fourth sheet gave the name of a state-run book shop on the outskirts of the city, on the Tula Road, describing items obtainable at the shop. None of the items were books, but items known to be used in espionage. Sheets following gave instructions on how the items should be assembled and used.

It shocked Chukotev. Someone, incredibly, had managed to get his system of distribution messed up. The stars only knew who they should have been destined for, but they had found their way to him and he couldn't report them while the place was in an uproar. There was a final sheet; on it were the names again, with pencilled alongside payments in American dollars. Mercy! He shuddered. Not only was there a spy-ring operating somewhere in the Directorate, there was a paymaster among them!

Chukotev lay for hours in bed without sleeping. He had to think of a way of reporting the information without becoming involved himself. He had too much all of a sudden and if the KGB got hold of it they would have him locked up while investigations took place. That could take weeks, months; in the meantime his entire family would become tainted people. They would lose their good jobs, their fine apartments and dachas, their permits to shop in the special shops – their cars. They would become non-people. He couldn't do that to them.

He could destroy the information and say nothing, but that would still not solve the problem of a traitorous ring at large somewhere. And, if someone were caught, made to give information, they might say they sent the money and papers to him by mistake. Then where would he be?

He could wait and hope for someone to be arrested. Then he could leap forward with the vital information and claim to have been doing a little investigation on his own. It would nail the culprit, make him into a hero, but he would have to have first-hand knowledge of when an arrest was made and that didn't always happen. One way or another he was forced into a very delicate position.

Grest had Andrei Chernigov followed for four days before he pounced. Chernigov held a respected position in the Foreign Ministry. A privileged member of the party, he required no special permits to travel abroad since all or most of his work took him to foreign countries. He had a lot of influence with the Supreme Soviet when it came to foreign policy. On his advice military experts were sent undercover to Vietnam, Angola and Mozambique; even to the Red Brigade in Italy and the IRA in Ireland. His advice had the West in a turmoil. Few questioned his judgement, but he was the man who admired the Great Wall of China while in conversation with Balquidder.

On the fifth day Grest struck. Chernigov had done nothing untoward in the days before. In fact Grest doubted if Chernigov ever did anything untoward while in Moscow. But Balquidder had given him the clue, even if it was to take the heat off his own man. It was something he had to act on.

Chernigov protested most vehemently when told he was under arrest, but the men under Grest's command ignored the protests; they took Grest's orders and nothing would prevent them doing their duty. They took Chernigov quickly to Kazator, inside the interrogation centre long before anyone

172

knew he'd been arrested. Grest's first question was a simple one.

'Why did you praise the Chinese enemy?'

The question meant nothing to Chernigov, but gradually it was explained to him. Questions were fired at him from a battery of interrogators: He was a Chinese spy; he had betrayed the Soviet people and the state ...

Chernigov resisted the questions, retorting with venom well into the night. The torturing began when dawn broke. He roared with anger when one by one his finger and toe-nails were ripped off; he tried to throw off his persecutors. Anger was replaced with pain and terror when they broke each one of his fingers, then his toes, but he fought on; nothing would make him confess to being a traitor ... until they nailed his left testicle to a wooden table.

Chernigov flowed with information after that. He never imagined there could be so much pain. He gave Grest names and dates, dates going back twenty years; he told how the information he traded was used against the Soviet Union. He couldn't stop once he'd started.

When it was over he was an old man.

Later that day KGB agents swept through Moscow in fast cars to addresses in a score of different streets. Men and women were beaten up on the spot and arrested; dragged away moaning or screaming to Kazator to face torture, trial and death. Before the day was out an entire Chinese spy-ring was rounded up.

Chernigov was given the best medical treatment Russia could offer. He was the leader; the dirty imperialist spy – the bandit chief. He would stand before a Soviet court.

A third courier, frightened by the events concerning the arrest of an entire Chinese spy-ring, approached his superior with the note he believed was put into his pocket by an Oriental. His superior telephoned Grest.

'Why did you not come forward sooner?' Grest said to the courier later.

The courier gave the statutory reply – fear.

Grest dismissed him to Kazator. Whether or not he was a spy was neither here nor there. He would be interrogated thoroughly and lose his job. What happened to him would be a lesson to others.

Capuchin was disturbed by the arrests. It was the talk of every department. And it escalated with gossip. People recounted incidents where colleagues had done or said something out of turn. He'd done nothing, but every hint would be followed up and it only wanted someone who didn't like him to say a wrong word. The KGB would have no trouble getting information from him.

But the enormity of the spy-ring shook him. Over sixty people had been arrested and taken to Kazator; taken from nearly every department within the government. Thankfully there had been none from his own section, but two had been taken from the 1st Directorate – those in charge had also been arrested. Twenty years it had gone on, they'd said. Now it was all over the world, flashed by the official news agency. Following release of the news all Chinese diplomats had been expelled at an hour's notice. That pleased him in a way for it kept Koong away from him, but there was still the chance that his name had been mentioned to someone in the spy-ring.

A negative approach to the possibility was something he couldn't afford to take. He would have been arrested by now had someone mentioned his name, but there was still time for that and he couldn't be around if it happened. He had to get out.

Which would be tricky. Travelling was banned. The only other way would be if he could drive north and slip across the Finnish frontier.

Twenty-Nine

'The couriers I've had the pleasure of speaking to,' said Grest to a Director, across the latter's desk. 'Tell me about them.'

'They are all ... they were all trusted members of the party — couriers with many year's standing. They were chosen for their discretion both here and abroad. They never drew attention to themselves ... in fact, they were the ideal people to have in one's employ.'

'Were they directly responsible to you?'

'Not to me personally as such. They took their instructions from me, but they were recruited by the courier service. When I required a new courier, I simply asked the service and they provided.'

'Yes, the head of the service said as much to me during his interrogation. How many do you have altogether?'

'Five.'

'The other two?'

'A man and a woman. They don't know each other so far as I know. Katherine Linski and Nikolai Malin.'

'Are they here at present?'

'They are on extended leave. They were told to stay home while the crisis was on.'

'They have not been in contact since?'

'Not for a few days ... I have their addresses if—'

'So have I, Comrade.' Grest rose, his face grim.

Chukotev let out a deep sigh when Grest left. He daren't now report the items sent to him. Linski and Malin probably had no more idea of the Chinese notes than he had, but since some of their colleaugues had had them, they were suspect. Everyone was suspect. He just daren't volunteer the packages.

Katherine Linski was still in bed when Grest and his men burst into her apartment. In bed with her was a bright-eyed youth, whose face registered shock when he saw the array of guns pointed at him. Katherine sat up in bed and demanded to know what was going on, just as photographs of them were taken. She screamed; the love-bites dotted about her pendulous breasts would be blown-up to show her decadence.

'Out!' Grest commanded. 'Stand in the middle of the room with your hands above your heads.'

Katherine jumped from the bed but the youth stayed behind, too scared to move, but he scrambled out when the barrel of a gun cracked against his nose.

'I want the note given to you by the Chinese spy,' Grest said with anger.

Pimples broke out over Katherine's body at the mention of the note. There was no use denying it and she pointed to her purse. Grest emptied it and pulled away the note. It was identical to the others.

'Move!' He shouted. 'You will be held for questioning.'

Katherine went first with her hands above her head. The youth followed, snivelling and begging to be allowed to go home. He was answered with a boot on his bare rear.

Grest went on to Malin's address. A glance inside the apartment told him what he wanted to know. Malin had left in a hurry. A message was relayed to KGB headquarters to have Malin's description circulated immediately. He had to be apprehended at all costs. Grest's suspicions were confirmed when a report came in informing him that a man answering the description had behaved in a furtive manner a week or so before.

That he was approaching the climax of his career, Grest was positive. Only the next day Comrade Makentov was to have special dispensation to travel to London, to escort home the man who could identify the English spy. Although he had nothing to go on yet, he felt sure that someone in the American ring would fall foul of him. In the evening he made his report to the Soviet.

In the conference centre there wasn't a spare seat to be had. As well as members of the Soviet, also attending were the Directors and section heads of the two Directorates. Everyone was nervous.

The Chairman called for silence.

'Comrades,' his voice was low and serious; he was still in shock. 'I have no doubt you realise the gravity of the present situation. Sixty-seven Chinese agents were caught in Comrade Grest's swoop. Some way or another, directly or indirectly, every government department is involved. The damage is irreparable. Each one of us is to blame; there can be no exceptions ... even our glorious President, Comrade Brezhnev, has written his apologies to the Soviet for not insisting on more stringent security precautions. We have been too soft; too soft with the imperialist nations and too soft with our own nationals. By being soft we have allowed the nation to drop into an apathy towards security. Too many people speak out of turn – drawn towards the dirty money waved in their faces by the warmongers. This must be stamped out. We must keep the warmongers out of our country, but we must have them begging to trade with us. As for our own; these traitorous swine who would betray Mother Russia; they must be destroyed; there must be no repetition of meeting people from the West. From henceforth, therefore, it will be considered a crime against the state to speak to anyone from the West. There will be no more dining or socialising with staff and families from foreign embassies unless specifically ordered to do so by the Soviet ...'

'There is another matter which must be brought into the open now, and that is the reason why you directors and section heads have been invited to join this conference. Comrade Grest will explain ...'

Grest rose to his feet, walked round the long table slowly, staring at each man in turn.

'We have uncovered a vast conspiracy to undermine the security of the Soviet Union. Our traditional enemies, the Chinese, infiltrated every government department ...' He went over old ground. 'But they are no more. However ...' He leaned over the table to let everyone see his face. 'The dangers are not yet past us. I have absolute proof that there are spy-rings in the

177

pay of the English and Americans operating under our very noses, right here in the Kremlin. Their days are numbered, for I expect a lead on the American ring in the next day or two. And tomorrow Comrade Makentov will depart for London to escort home someone who will identify the controller of the English spy-ring. But that is not all ...'

Grest watched their faces. They were expecting a climax of some kind. A different speaker rose. Everyone turned their heads. Comrade Lukoteski suddenly spoke from further along the table.

Lukoteski was a military representative on the Soviet; renowned for his harshness and cruelty. He was KGB, always a member of the military wing of the KGB; but officially an army marshal. Like many others he'd followed Stalin's orders to eliminate those who had seen the West at the end of the war; by his own hand he'd executed his own staff so that they could not tell what they'd seen.

'There is,' said Lukoteski, 'the matter of where the English spy operates and his position within the Kremlin. I have had long talks with Comrade Grest and I agree one-hundred per cent with his suspicions. There can be no other explanation — that is, the English spy, code-named 'K', we believe ... is one of you!'

No one moved or spoke.

'It has to be one of you. Comrade Grest discovered our mistake. Our mistake was having all Directors in here at the same time at the morning meeting, instead of having them separately. You Directors had every opportunity to gather information that you were not entitled to know, to use it against the Soviet people. That alone condemns one of you ... And not forgetting our section heads; you no doubt talk over with your Directors the minutes of the morning meetings. This is an area in which we have been too soft, and I can assure you that nothing of the same will occur again.

'But that does not rule out the members of the Soviet. Any member of the Soviet could be an English spy; they are better placed than anyone to obtain information. No matter who he is, he is a condemned man. Until he is found and brought to trial I want the guilty party to think. I want him to think about

178

his wife and children; his grandchildren if he has any. ...'

Nikolai Malin was more miserable than ever. It was his intention to escape and the longer he stayed with Lena Molodechno the slender his chances were becoming. His only way out was via the American Embassy; he'd been along to it two days previous only to find it discreetly surrounded with KGB. He'd no disire to go back to the Chinese, not after the hours of thought he'd given to Koong. Moscow had a morbid fear of the Chinese and it had rubbed off on him.

Lena was bleeding him dry of his money. She didn't go out to work, just stayed at home urging him to stay with her, to renew their old friendship. It got on his nerves but he'd nowhere else to go. Fifty dollars a day it was costing him. They ate well, and Lena had expensive clothing in her wardrobe again. He hated thinking about what would happen when his money ran out.

Lena hurried home from her latest shopping trip. Malin was lying on the old sofa when she rushed in. He didn't turn his head; he was laughing for the first time in days. The clowns on the variety on TV momentarily made him forget his predicament.

'Get out!' Lena screemed at him, her face masked with fear, tears threatening to burst from her eyes.

Her sudden shout made him jump. 'What's wrong?'

'Get out! ... Leave! ... Right this minute!'

Lena began running around the apartment finding his clothes. She threw them at him, trembling, her bottom lip flapping. Her eyes were as big as plates.

'What's wrong, Lena?'

'Wrong?' Lena whimpered. 'The KGB are looking all over the city for you and you ask me what's wrong! Get your clothes on and get out. Don't come back here and don't say you've been here!'

'I've nowhere to go.' He pleaded.

'I don't care!' Lena started to throw her arms about, pushing him towards the door. 'Find somewhere! I can't have you here a minute longer!'

'But, Lena ...'

'Jesus Christian Christ! Don't you hear me? The KGB are after you. They have your photograph on notices all over Moscow. Are you listening? K-G-B!'

Malin pulled on the rest of his clothing. He would have to leave or her shouts would draw attention.

'I must have something to eat and drink.'

'Take it! Take it all!' Lena pushed the shopping bag at him.

Malin took a bottle of vodka from the bag and drank a mouthful. He was shaking more than Lena.

'Get out!' Lena was sobbing.

Malin dreaded the streets now. Snow was falling heavier than ever, piling up against walls. People were about, shopping for the next day, but soon they would be indoors; he would be on his own, vulnerable. He wished he had a better pair of shoes, boots preferably, for the snow quickly softened the imitation leather of the shoes he'd bought in the West.

The cold was intense, more so following the warmth of Lena's apartment. Before long it bit through his outer clothing. Keeping to the side streets, away from the brighter-lit thoroughfares, he began to wander, with no specific destination in mind. He stopped once to eat some of the sausage Lena had bought, tearing at it with chattering teeth and looking this way and that for the bulky figures of the KGB. He'd never known such fear.

The streets cleared for two hours, becoming crowded again between eleven and twelve when the late-shift workers would make their way home. He envied them. They were not appointed to jobs where they had to watch for their lives. They could be given a job; they would do it and be given comforts in return. If they did it wrong they were admonished like children, but they went on living their lives. If he did wrong he was a criminal.

Midnight was long past when he stopped for a drink. It flowed down his throat easily, filling him with warmth, giving him the urge to go on. He took bearings, estimating where he was, but his mind was confused with fear and alcohol, making it difficult to gauge distances to anywhere.

The night grew even colder. Only the odd person was at large and when a police car passed on its rounds he was forced to take cover, convinced they were looking for no one else but him.

He stumbled into a high wooden fence. Looking up he could make out a new apartment block in the process of being constructed. It was empty and forbidding, but somewhere in its innards he would find a place to sleep. He found a way through the fence and stopped dead. Voices were somewhere ahead; low mumbling voices; someone was chuckling; there was the crash of broken glass, then the sound of a fist on flesh.

He guessed what the voices were. They were the tramps of Moscow. They did not officially exist but there were many of them. They were his kind now. Walking softly through the snow and rubble on the building site, he stooped to pass underneath a low doorway. There was a fire glowing; the talking stopped.

'Welcome, brother,' said a man by the fire. 'You look cold.'

Malin nodded and came closer to the fire. They were Jews, driven to alcoholism by the persecution of the KGB and the Soviet.

'You look like a man in trouble,' said another. Again Malin nodded.

'Sit,' said the first speaker. 'We have a drink to warm you.'

Someone handed him a bottle of wine. It was rough, stung the back of his throat, but grateful for any helping hand he swallowed some. It wasn't strong enough for him and he took a half-empty bottle of vodka from the shopping bag. The others watched with envy while he drank from it, then smiled when he passed it on.

'A welcome sinner,' one of the Jews said. 'Do you have any food?'

'Yes, here ...' Malin was anxious to be friendly. Maybe the Jews would know a way to get out. Keeping some sausage and bread for himself, the rest he gave to the others.

There were five of them, four men and a woman, each one of them in a pitiable state. What could only be described as rags were wrapped round their thin bodies.

A second bottle of vodka found its way round the group, emptied in minutes.

'You will be safe here,' said the man who'd spoken first; he

181

introduced himself as Josef. 'Work has been postponed on this site for two weeks.'

'How do you know?'

Because they cannot get certain building materials ...' The others laughed. 'A certain material they use happens to be our bread and water.'

'Oh?'

'Yes, brother. We steal it, sell it to others who also cannot wait for the few supplies available. They pay us a pittance but it keeps us from dying. Are you comfortable?'

'Yes thank you.'

'Come closer to the fire. Soon your body will be warm then you can sleep peacefully. One of us always stands guard so you can sleep without fear of being caught in a raid.'

'Thank you. You are the first people who have given me some help without asking to be paid.'

Josef nodded. 'We know, brother. That is why we help each other. Without each other we would perish.'

Malin thanked them again and lay down closer to the fire. The heat was getting to him, his body becoming warm. He felt sleepy.

When he woke in the morning he was cold. He sat up, shivered and looked at the fire. Only a few embers of wood were still glowing. The Jews were gone.

He needed a cigarette. Automatically his hand went to a pocket. He had no pockets! He was dressed in rags! his clothes were gone ... his papers ... his shoes ... his money ... everything. ...

Malin dropped to his knees. His hands were numbed, his body shook from cold. He cursed while trying to re-kindle the fire. He cursed the Soviet government for creating a regime that thrived on fear; the Americans for having approached him those years before; the government again for persecuting the Jews who stole his money – the Jews for stealing it.

The fire burst into flame and he began to giggle.

Thirty

News of the mass arrests took the world by surprise and the Peking government recalled many diplomats from other countries to review their system of espionage. It shattered Huan in Paris; his only consolation believing that no one yet knew about Malin and Capuchin.

The Vicar was satisfied to a certain extent. Grest would never admit to his superiors that his information which led to the arrests came from London. That kept London clear of any blame and would make the Americans even more worried. All parties were aware now that the Americans stirring up too much dirt in the first place had started it all off. But Kocker wasn't safe yet.

There were protests in London and other cities throughout Britain following the mass arrests. The giant deal was signed between London and Peking, in the circumstances making Peking a friend, and having friends arrested enmasse was insulting. Guilty or not the suspects would never be given a fair trial – was the consensus of opinion – yet one of the men who would undoubtedly bear some of the responsibility for their deaths was having the red carpet laid out for him on his visit to London. It was a travesty of justice and human morals to have the man – now dubbed by some newspapers as 'the butcher' – in London while his underlings tortured sixty-odd unfortunate Russians. The protesters wanted the visit stopped.

When Makentov arrived at Heathrow Airport protesters greeted him. Police held them back but they could not stop the hail of beer-cans that showered the tar-mac and carpet paving his path to the arrival hall.

Among the crowds, shouting and swearing, were several of

Balquidders' people, with orders never to let Makentov out of their sight, to report every movement however small he would make. In three days George Trayner was to be released.

Capuchin made his mind up. Lukoteski's tirade convinced him that the only path open to him was to cross the Finnish border. Someone among the Chinese spy-ring was sure to mention his name sooner or later.

And he'd have to move quickly. It would have to be practically non-stop, for it would be impossible to stop on the way. His car had a range of 300 miles and 500 miles to the Finnish frontier added to the problem. Spare cans of petrol in the boot would solve it as long as no one stopped him for questioning. Considering everything there was, it would be a miracle if he made it.

But he had no choice.

Makentov was made comfortable in his hotel room in London's Park Lane when Malin crept out of the building site where he'd taken refuge. The day had been agony without food and something to drink; without the fire he would have died. The Jews hadn't returned.

The night was the same as the one previous; cold, bitter cold. Snow was falling like it was finding its true home. Shuffling through it he knew what he'd have to do; he'd heard about it often enough in the West.

After midnight his struck. A pretty girl was making her way home from work. She never heard him rush up behind her and before she could gather her wits his arm was around her throat, flicking her to the ground in a single movement. A fist in her mouth prevented the scream from coming, but she began to fight, thumping him with her gloved hands and trying to kick him in the groin. Malin was desperate. They were in a main street; anyone could come along – police or public they would come after him – he couldn't afford to be merciful. He pounded his fists into her face until her resistance ceased, snatched her handbag and ran.

In the entrance to a building due for demolition he knelt on the ground to search the handbag. The first thing he found was

184

a packet of East German cigarettes and a Czech lighter, then the money. Twenty two roubles and a few kopecks; not a fortune, but sufficient to keep him alive for a day or two.

The girl's blood was on the rags protecting his body, but it was the least of his worries when entering one of the all-night shops. The lone shop assistant served him, but did it quickly, with disdain, hurrying him out before anyone decent came in. She went to the telephone immediately but he didn't care; he had food and cheap vodka. They would keep him going until the next day. But he also needed some clothing.

Following a quick meal and a copious amount of vodka he went on the prowl again, looking for another girl victim – he didn't feel like tackling a man.

The girl was carrying a sports bag under her arm, possibly returning from a night of netball or something. She was in a hurry, not too far away from the building sight.

Fortified with vodka Malin jumped on her, clamping a dirty hand across her mouth and lifting her off the ground with the other. She struggled, kicking, but Malin let it happen, staggering backwards until he reached the opening that took him into the building site. He half-turned, forcing the girl's feet to drag on the ground, driven on by desperation, pulling her over the rubble towards the fire.

The girl was sobbing and gasping, her blue eyes filled with terror. Malin pulled the furlined hood from her head and for a second was ashamed; she was no more than seventeen. His shame disappeared when she opened her mouth to scream. Twice his fist came down, breaking her jaw. She remained still while he removed her clothing.

He didn't notice her shapely body; it was her clothes he wanted. He dressed himself in all her clothing except her brassiere. The clothes were much his size and he'd little trouble getting them on. Panties, tights, ankle-socks and underslip, it didn't matter. They were warm clothing; with her insulated trousers and coat on top no one would know what he had on underneath. Only the shoes gave him trouble; they were a size too small.

The girl just lay there, choking painfully on sobs, her belly heaving. Her eyes stared directly above her, unblinking and wide.

Malin warmed almost immediately. The furlined coat shut out the bitter cold and a fresh supply of wood on the fire brought a cosiness to his situation. With more vodka inside him the future looked better. As soon as it was light, or perhaps when the streets were busy, he'd go back to the American embassy and try to get inside. All he had to do was get across the threshold of the gate; once over he would be safe. Then it would be plain sailing to America – money, freedom.

He dozed off dreaming of America, waking with a start when something cracked. His heart missed a beat, ready to run off if the men he feared had found him. It was only the girl. She was still lying where he'd thrown her, but somehow one of her arms had got into the fire. It seemed to be melting. At closer inspection he saw it was ice. The girl was frozen stiff. Dead.

He went to sleep.

It wasn't so bad in the morning. The warm clothes had kept him from becoming too cold during the night. He rose, blowing on the glowing embers of the fire to bring it back to life, piling lumps of wood on top. Vodka warmed his inside; the food was solid but on chewing it became eatable. It made him feel better. The girl resembled a frosted log move than a human being. The arm was still in the fire, burned away to a black stump, while the rest of her was covered with a centimetre of frost and ice. Her eyes were still open.

He went unnoticed in the street. Comparatively well-dressed his dirty features were hidden beneath the furlined hood. The vodka gave him the courage to travel and he jumped on the first bus that came along, twenty minutes later getting off close to the America Embassy.

From a vantage point Malin studied the embassy. It was already a hive of activity. Men and women were coming and going. Outside were uniformed guards of the KGB, supposedly there to prevent riotous Muscovites from causing any kind of trouble. No one was fooled, though. He was in no doubt there would be plain clothed agents in the area also.

It was so near. All he had to do was get inside and identify himself.

From along the street came a man who was obviously an American. He carried a bag in one hand, swinging the other, whistling. No Russian felt happy enough to whistle.

Malin crossed the wide street and fell into step with the American.

'Listen,' he said, panic in his voice. 'My name is Nikolai Malin, known to the CIA as Jesuit. I must get out of Russia …'

'Get the hell out of here!' Will Oram snapped. Christ! He had a hundred of them every day.

They were nearing the embassy.

'I work for the CIA!' Malin was nearly in tears. 'I am known as Jesuit and my contact—'

'Piss off, willyah!' Oram snarled, calling to one of the guards. 'Hey! Can't you get this bum off my back?'

From all over men came, civilian and uniformed, from doorways and street corners, all waving guns and shouting for him to stop. Malin found a rifle pointed at him. It was useless; the Americans didn't believe him. He had to run.

The dead girl failed him. Her boots, with slightly high-heels, prevented him from running. They didn't know how.

They were on him, pinning him to the ground. It was the end, but with a last, sudden burst of defiance, he yelled out to the Americaw:

'Tell them Capuchin "does" work for Peking! Tell them Jesuit found out!'

A rifle butt crashed down on his head and the world went black.

'What was all that about, Will?' Oram was asked when he got inside the embassy.

'Oh, just some guy who thought he could get to the States.'

'Did you know him?'

'Nah! Never seen him before. But he shouted a message. I don't know if it'll mean anything to anyone.'

'Tell me and I'll check with Washington.'

Malin was immediately taken to Kazator where, stripped naked, the girl's clothes became evident. He'd no resistance left. The thought of being tortured terrified him and at little insistence from Grest he readily told the KGB tape-recorders everything they wanted to hear.

With a posse of agents Grest went for Capuchin. Cars

surrounded the apartment block where he lived, an agent confirmed that his car was in its normal parking space, another that someone was in the apartment. In the back seat of the car were suitcases and piles of documents, and in the boot several containers filled with petrol.

Capuchin lived on the fifth floor and although Grest and his men padded silently up each single step, the occupants of some of the apartments seemed to sense something was happening. They made sure their doors were locked; turning up the volume on their radios and TVs to drown out any screams that might come after.

On the fifth cloor Grest nodded. Shots were fired and the lock on Capuchin's door burst, the force throwing the door back on its hinges. Grest led the way and the others piled in behind him, spreading around the room.

Sitting on the floor in front of the fireplace were Karol Zobovic and Marya Lus.

'Good evening, Comrade'. Grest said softly, grimly. 'Comrade Capuchin.'

By dawn Grest learned that Zobovic and Lus had misled everyone. They had never forgiven the Soviet and KGB for insisting they divorce their spouses years before, planning revenge. Zobovic had already been taken into the CIA's clutches and when he put the same proposition to Lus she readily agreed. Working together they were able to compile information from signals entering and leaving the Kremlin, milking the KGB of secrets. News of their arrest was then given to the world.

Rogal went into a fury.

'That bastard Balquidder gave him away, Chief!' He snapped at Mellini.

'It looks that way, Ray,' Mellini conceded, 'but let's wait and see what happened. We only have Moscow's word they've been lifted.'

'Jesus!' Rogal couldn't get over it.

'Maybe he was working for the Reds, Ray. Could've been caught because of that.'

'Jesus!'

Thirty-One

A neighbour called the police complaining of the smell coming from the apartment. The door was broken down and Bryant's body found just as Kocker had left it. The investigating policeman vaguely recognised Bryant from his description. He called the KGB and Grest was wakened from his sleep.

It was Grest's day of triumph. The apartment was searched from top to bottom; a wealth of espionage information revealed itself. Beside the radio set on the list of frequencies there were five frequencies the BBC used in its French broadcasts; and Grest knew that when the broadcast ended the empty frequencies were used for a few minutes to transmit coded morse signals to English agents operating in the countries aligned to the Warsaw Pact. He went on with unconcealed glee.

Nothing was overlooked, the cookery book bringing howls of delight from his normally serious mouth. Somewhere in each page containing a photograph was a name and a location – the name on the very first page being Leonev Chukotev.

American dollars and English pounds worth thousands of roubles on the black market were discovered taped to the underside of the wardrobe; underneath the lip of the toilet bowl was a large sheet, folded small, sealed in a plastic bag, with a 'family tree' written on it. At the top of the tree was Leonev Chukotev.

Grest's chest was bursting with pride. In the space of a few days he'd broken three major spy rings, capturing their controllers into the bargain. Chukotev was not yet in custody, but that was a mere formality.

The names were rounded up, including the apartment's

resident. Grest stayed on until apartments nearby were searched as a matter of routine; and one of his men wiped clean the windows of the snow-covered car.

Grest rushed to the street to see the damning evidence his men found. There was a name, Peter Nevsky, and Grest could place his face.

Even under torture Chukotev protested. He was innocent of any treason, he screamed, but a search of his house brought forth enough evidence to hang him several times over. Chukotev could protest all he liked. Grest knew that in the end he would confess to being the highly placed English spy he'd been seeking. Everyone confessed eventually and Chukotev would be no different.

Peter Nevsky broke down with a minimum of torture, revealed the names of the Carmelite group. Once again the news agencies of the world buzzed with the reports. Sixty-seven Chinese agents had been caught, forty-seven in the American Carmelite group and 133 from an English group, one of whom had penetrated deep into the Kremlin. It shook the free world.

The Vicar sighed with relief when the news broke. Ninety per cent of his work was done.

'Colin,' he said into the secret telephone network. 'It's time for the last act. Have Trayner released at once; he's got to be out of the country before Makentov realises he's been released. You know what's to be done?'

'Yes, sir.'

In Moscow, Lukoteski was raving. Had he not warned the Soviet?

Kocker was thinking the same as the Vicar. Only ninety per cent of the work was done.

Thirty-Two

'Christ, Ray!' Joe Mellini was raging. 'The God-damned Carmelites. I told you they shouldn't have been used.'

'Jeez, chief,' Rogal pleaded for forgiveness. 'Neither of us thought they'd be taken.'

'We've lost everything! It'll take years to build up anything like it again.'

'There's still the Cistercians ...'

'Cistercians? What good will they be? It'll be a long time before they gain positions of influence. Jesus, Ray, you didn't half foul this one up.'

A secretary pushed her head round the door.

'A Mr Balquidder to see you, Mr Mellini ...'

'Shit! Not him ... Okay, show him in, kid.'

Balquidder wasn't smiling but he was the gentleman as always. Only with Mellini, however. He behaved as if Rogal wasn't there.

'I haven't come at an inopportune moment?'

'Not at all, Colin,' said Mellini. 'Take a seat.'

Balquidder nodded and sat down.

'What can we do for you, Colin?'

'Very little, Mr Mellini, I'm afraid ...' The use of the official title wasn't lost on either American. It was no social call. 'Some weeks ago you imagined you found something – fictitious information we were supposed to have given you by mistake. You sent one of your colleagues to see me, to sound me out about the supposed affair. From that moment on you made a song and dance about it; enough song and dance to make our friends in Moscow take an interest in us. You will be well aware that my government lost 133 agents in Russia – a disaster for our security – and whether you like it or not you were solely responsible.'

Mellini nodded. 'Yeah, I concede the point. But we thought you were giving us away to save your own guy, and we wanted to know who your guy was. Okay, so we were wrong. We can only apologise; there's nothing we can do to reverse the situation. Yeah, it was our fault.'

'Quite. Your Ambassador and President are falling over themselves to apologise.'

'What can I say, Colin?' Mellini was ill at ease.

'I had a conversation with your Mr Rogal not so long ago. I informed him that if he did not refrain from sticking his nose into business that did not concern him, and having my people killed, I would arrange for his family to attend a bereavement. Your Mr Rogal not only chose to ignore my advice, but also found it acceptable to have 133 of my government's employees arrested, to face certain death. My advice still stands. Mr Rogal was given fair warning. If the fellow is not out of the country in four hours time, his family will be attending a bereavement ...'

Balquidder rose, making for the door.

'In future, Mr Mellini, my government will expect you to inform her when anyone employed by the CIA wishes to visit Britain.'

'Now, just a minute! We don't expect you—'

Balquidder held up his hand.

'Just until we are certain you can be trusted, Mr Mellini.' For the first time in the conversation Balquidder smiled. He was gone before they could react.

Both Mellini and Rogal were on the next plane to Washington. Similar words had passed between Ambassadors and the President felt ashamed and humiliated. Someone had to pay.

The double-agent Boris Petrokovic was buried in a quiet cemetery in the North-East of England under an assumed name, and the couple who had killed Penton in Finland were buried in a double grave in Devon. Moscow and Washington weren't told.

George Trayner was released against his will. He had been

given a date, but his release came two days early. Nor did he like the look of the two men who came to witness his release. They were secret-service men or he was the President of the USA.

'Hello, Mr Trayner,' said the taller of the two. 'I'm Johnnie Taylor, and my friend here is Eddie Hislop. We will be your escorts.'

'What do you mean escorts? I don't need you blokes.'

'Orders, Mr Trayner. You are to be released a little earlier than expected.'

'So, where am I going with you?'

'A little place in the country, one might say … or perhaps along the coast.'

'I'm not going. I'm staying here until friends come to pick me up.'

Trayner's friends were from the Russian embassy. It was all arranged that he would be picked up at a certain time two days hence.

'On the contrary, Mr Trayner. You will come with us.'

Trayner studied them. Taylor was six-two at least. He had a pleasant face and shoulder length hair. Young, he was not too well built muscle-wise, but underneath Trayner reckoned he'd be a dangerous man. Hislop was shorter, broader and stockier, again with shoulder length hair, but with a sly, cruel face. He was the one jingling the wrist-bracelets.

'Just do everything we say, Mr Trayner,' said Hislop, 'and you'll come to no harm. 'Fraid I'll have to attach you to me, though.'

There was nothing Trayner could do. He wondered if there was a remote chance of them knowing his secret.

In London another three men were together; in a car on its way to Southend Airport. All three sat in the back, none of them speaking; the chauffeur in front quietly listened to the radio. At the airport they were taken away from the public entrance, to an empty warehouse, where, changing cars they drove out to a private plane waiting to take off. The plane had a crew of two, neither of whom showed themselves, but spoke to their passengers over the intercom. Their destination was

Rotterdam.

Taylor and Hislop had a car waiting for Trayner, not outside the prison as was normal, but inside, pointed at the small gates used to move out the prison's garbage.

'In you get, please, Mr Trayner,' said Hislop.

Trayner had no choice. He was manacled to Hislop and Hislop was giving him a look that told him there would be trouble if he didn't.

When they drove through the small gates, Taylor driving, an identical car picked up three men outside the main gates and drove off. One of the three had his head covered with a blanket.

Trayner didn't see much of the outside world for some time. For the first ten miles after leaving the gate he was forced to lie on the floor with Hislop on top of him. Not until Taylor was certain they weren't being followed was he allowed to get up.

'Where are we going?'

'Somewhere nice,' said Hislop.

'I want my solicitor. He was supposed to meet me on my release.'

'You're not released yet.'

'This isn't right.'

'Shut up.'

'Pardon?'

'I said "shut up"!' Hislop turned to snarl at Trayner. 'Shut up if you don't want a smack in the teeth.'

When the plane arrived in Rotterdam a car with blacked-out windows was waiting. All three men climbed in. Still none of them spoke, although the man sandwiched by the other two desperately wanted to ask questions. The driver of the car didn't turn his head once. He knew exactly where to go.

Trayner lifted himself out of his seat when he saw their destination. He recognised Harwich, a major terminal for channel-crossing ferries.

'What ...' he began.

'Just leave everything to us,' said Hislop.

The ferry was in darkness and except for a solitary

194

policeman no one was in sight.

'This way, Mr Trayner.'

The car drove off and Taylor spoke to the policeman, nodding as the other spoke. Following a final nod from Taylor, Trayner was led up the gangway.

Someone in uniform met them at the top, escorted them to a cabin without a word and left them. Another uniform appeared; Trayner noticed the rank of chief officer.

'There will be no need to leave the cabin. As you can see it has its own toilet and shower. Anything you need will be brought to you. We should berth at the Hook of Holland at 06.00, but you won't be able to disembark until 07.30. The last passenger should be off by 07.00, so half-an-hour should be plenty of time to let them get away.'

'That'll suit us fine,' Taylor nodded.

The officer left and Trayner was manacled to a steel rail at the head of his bunk. He was forced to lie on his side and to ensure that he couldn't climb out – but still allowing him to be comfortable, one of his ankles was manacled to a rail at the bottom of the bunk. Taylor stripped down to his underclothes, climbed onto one of the other three bunks and went to sleep. Hislop lay down, but his eyes never left Trayner. It was another hour before the sounds of the first passengers arriving could be heard.

Trayner tried not to sleep but eventually he did and in the morning found a fresh change of clothing laid out for him.

'Shower and shave,' said Hislop, 'and put these on.'

There was a smart pair of white slacks, a dark-blue blazer with a badge on the pocket Trayner couldn't place, black shoes and a white polo-necked sweater.

'They aren't my clothes.'

Hislop was ready. 'Must I tell you again? Shut up or get a smack in the teeth ... And we wouldn't want to mess up your gentleman's clothes now, would we?'

Trayner was mystified about what was going on Nor did he trust any of it.

Their train left for Rotterdam at 08.00, and since most of the ship's passengers had left on earlier trains they virtually had it to themselves: Until Schiedam and Vlaardigen when hordes of provincial commuters herded on.

The later editions of the London dailies published the unexpected news that Trayner had been released two days early. He wanted no publicity, he was reported as saying, and asked permission of the Home Secretary to be given an early release date. The Home Secretary had obliged, keeping his release secret until he was on his way out of the country. It took everyone by surprise.

On the third floor of a building overlooking Rotterdam's main railway station, the three men were watching from a window.

'It's time,' said one.

The man always between the other two was forced to the floor. A needle was pushed into his arm. He tried to fight it, stiffening against it, but it found its way into a vein and after a few minutes his body relaxed.

'How do you feel, squire?' one of the other two said.

'Marvellous!'

'You know what to do?'

'Yes, I think so. But you'd better go over it once more.'

'Okay, squire ...'

Taylor and Hislop let the other passengers leave the train before leaving themselves. They walked to the ticket barrier, presented their tickets, thanked the collector and strolled onto the concourse with Trayner between them.

'That's it, Mr Trayner,' said Hislop, unlocking the manacles. 'You're free now.'

'What?' Trayner was taken by surprise.

'Don't you want to be free?' Taylor handed him his identification.

'That's the way out ...' Hislop pointed. 'Any taxi-driver will take you to the Soviet consulate.'

Before Trayner could say another word the two men walked off and disappeared into the crowds. He looked down at the papers in his hand, the small wad of Dutch guilders, shaking his head with amazement.

Pieter Wiersma, a Dutch national, but also a colonel in the KGB, gasped when Trayner emerged from the station. The

British Home Office had caused a flap in the early hours of the morning when it informed the Russian Embassy of Trayner's release. It was totally unexpected, brought on, the Home Secretary had said, because word had reached London that Washington was interested in Trayner. The reason for the interest was not known, but since London had struck a bargain with Moscow she felt obliged to honour the bargain to the best of her ability. Trayner was therefore released early and given passage to the Continent.

The London embassy immediately sent word across the Channel; agents in all the cross-channel ports were roused from their beds and instructed to keep watch. Although Trayner's information about the English spy was now obsolete, trust and loyalty were at stake. The British had honoured their part of the bargain; Trayner was released; the American's hadn't been informed, and once on the Continent he was Moscow's responsibility. If Moscow couldn't look after him, many agents would no longer trust their masters. Wiersma hadn't for a moment expected to see him in Rotterdam.

Looking through the telescopic sight he caressed the rifle. It was a tribute to man's achievement; a beautiful piece of workmanship. He'd never felt happier.

Then he saw him; the chap with the white slacks and dark blue blazer. He stood out, looking bewildered outside the station. And there was the tell-tale badge.

He took careful aim, remembering what his two friends told him, squeezing the trigger when the sights lined up with the badge. There was a bark, he squeezed again, clearly seeing the dark spots on the badge and the chap's forehead.

He stood up.

Traffic came to a halt, women screamed, Wiersma gasped a second time and raced across the road. More screams followed and the crowd rapidly gathering made a path for the man carrying the rifle.

He was smiling. His instructions were to check his kill. If the man was not dead he was to finish him. He could see nothing but the man he'd shot; the people around him were non-existent, shut out by the massive drug dosage. The man was

197

dead.

Someone tackled him, fetching him to the ground. Wiersma joined in, feeling into the pockets for identification. Police were pushing their way through the crowd.

Wiersma found the name. It was as they'd feared. He handed the papers to a policeman, at the same time taking a pen from his own pocket. The top of the pen came away easily, revealing a four-inch long steel needle.

'It says his name's Edward Anderson.' His flourish of the papers hid his other hand. 'An American CIA agent.'

His other hand pushed the needle into Anderson's heart, withdrew it, pushed it against his arm and stood. The crowd was pushing closer, the police were calling for them to get back. Wiersma went back slowly, edging through the crowd, vanishing from sight to make his report. He would be long gone before Anderson's cause of death was established. In minutes it would be released to the world that a CIA agent had murdered Trayner.

'A punitive revenge,' said Grest. 'As it was, we didn't need Trayner.'

'Which just goes to show that the British Secret Service is ridden with American agents.' Lukoteski said.

Lukoteski had been raging since the news of Trayner's death came in.

'I would make spies afraid to come to Russia. And I still don't trust the remainder of our section heads. I would execute them all!'

No one said anything. He was not a man to argue with. Lukoteski wanted to get rid of everyone working at the Directorates; to begin afresh; no one in his opinion was to be trusted. All eyes were on him as he turned to look out of a window. No one could see his face from that position ...

Makentov's visit was suddenly cancelled; cries of victory rang round the country. The protesters seemed to have won, and no one said anything to alter the impression. Public opinion had driven the butcher back to his den.

On the other side of the coin some trade unions threatened

the Government with a one-day strike to protest against the bad manners portrayed. The Russian was a guest of the trade unionists of Great Britain and it was a slap in the face to have the visit curtailed so bluntly after it had begun. The Government was caught in a cleft stick. It could not say the visit had been cancelled so abruptly on orders from the Russian Supreme Soviet.

Thirty-Three

'What the hell for?' Joe Mellini appealed to the head of the CIA. 'What in hell did they want to do that for? They'd lost their man. Jesus! What good did it do them to have Trayner killed?'

'Simple,' the head of the CIA said quietly. 'We appear to have been following the affair closer than you and agent Rogal. We believe London's man wasn't caught. It's logical. Trayner was the only person who could identify him so he had to be taken out. London took us ... took all of us on ... made pricks of us all. An elaborate plan, okay, but so skilful that the Russians could only believe its results. That guy, Grest, in Moscow, believes he broke three major spy-rings, that London came off worst. He'll never realise London came off best. That's why, Mellini — London is still top-dog! Until the Cistercians come of age we'll be going cap-in-hand to London, and we'll never really know what's going on.'

'What I don't understand,' said Rogal, 'is why, if they've had this guy in there for so many years, they've allowed Moscow to spy on them and steal vital information?'

The President spoke. 'I wish,' he smiled, 'I had the same guy. Moscow could spy until it was blue in the face, because I would be content with the knowledge that I knew everything. Why should London worry? No matter what Moscow steals, it can never steal more than it can use; and what it can use and what it has already got — London knows. London just knows. ...'

'So we've still got to get the guy. We've got to find him!'

'No chance.' The CIA chief shook his head. 'This has all happened because we tried once before. We can't risk it again. What's more, all reference to the affair has been deleted from the computer banks.'

'Wha ... How?'

'Because the God-damned English have a guy in here as well!' It was a snarl. 'A couple of days after you went to London, it all disappeared.'

'Jesus!'

'And, by the way. That leaflet you had so much trouble with. The guys here worked it out.'

'When?'

'Ages ago. It's been lying here since. It gave us an idea we were beaten, but there was nothing we could do about it when the Curtain came down.'

Mellini grabbed the paper the President handed him.

'Aw, shit!'

BARGAINS!!
NOTTINGHAM PEOPLES' EXECUTIVE.
RUMMAGE SALE AND FÊTE.
SATURDAY 17TH FEBRUARY 1968.
DAWSON HALL, ASH STREET.
1.30 PM.

Thirty-Four

A small paragraph in *The Times* announced that Mr Colin Balquidder had been awarded an OBE for his services to British Industry.

There was a much larger crowd saw Makentov off than saw him arrive. Anti-war, CND and other minor protest groups thronged the departure lounge long before his plane was due to leave. When he did arrive from London he was once again pelted with rubbish, but Makentov took it all in his stride. Like every Russian official he smiled a little and waved his hand. The crowds might have been cheering him.

The red carpet was strewn with rubbish, making him tread carefully along it. He turned suddenly, increasing the abuse and insults of the crowd. His eye caught, just for a brief instant, the eye of the old man at the front of the crowd. The old man put his thumb to his top row of teeth and flicked it forward casually.

Makentov did the same, only flicking his thumb forward quickly, seemingly with hatred and defiance, daring the crowd to attack him. The crowd roared its hatred in return, screaming for the blood of the man they called the butcher. But Makentov smiled, turning away. He'd acknowledged the message.

The Vicar also smiled. Erghizh Nijinsky Makentov, the man only the Vicar knew as Kocker ... was safe!

GENERAL FICTION

Δ	042616184X	CYRIL ABRAHAM **The Onedin Line: The High Seas**	**80p**
Δ	0426172671	**The Onedin Line: The Trade Winds**	**80p**
Δ	0352304006	**The Onedin Line: The White Ships**	**95p**
Δ	042697114X	**The Shipmasters**	**80p**
Δ	0352305738	BRUCE STEWART **The Onedin Line: The Turning Tide**	**£1.25**
	0352304251	TESSA BARCLAY **A Sower Went Forth**	**£1.50**
	0352302712	JUDY BLUME **Forever**	**75p***
	035230703X	ANDRÈ BRINK **A Dry White Season**	**£1.95**
	0352305916	**Rumours of Rain**	**£1.95**
	0352306904	**An Instant in the Wind**	**£1.95**
Δ	0352302747	MICHAEL J. BIRD **The Aphrodite Inheritance**	**85p**
	0352307773	ADRIAN BROOKS **The Glass Arcade**	**£1.50***
	0352303514	MAGDA CHEVAK **Splendour in the Dust**	**£1.50**
Δ	0352395621	JACKIE COLLINS **The Stud**	**£1.25**
	0352300701	**Lovehead**	**£1.25**
	0352398663	**The World is Full of Divorced Women**	**£1.25**
Δ	0352398752	**The World is Full of Married Men**	**75p**

* Not for sale in Canada. ● Reissues.
Δ Film & T.V. tie-ins.

STAR Books are obtainable from many booksellers and newsagents. If you have any difficulty please send purchase price plus postage on the scale below to:

Star Cash Sales
P.O. Box 11
Falmouth
Cornwall
OR
Star Book Service,
G.P.O. Box 29,
Douglas,
Isle of Man,
British Isles.

While every effort is made to keep prices low, it is sometimes necessary to increase prices at short notice. Star Books reserve the right to show new retail prices on covers which may differ from those advertised in the text or elsewhere.

Postage and Packing Rate
UK: 40p for the first book, 18p for the second book and 13p for each additional book ordered to a maximum charge of £1·49p. BFPO and EIRE: 40p for the first book, 18p for the second book, 13p per copy for the next 7 books, thereafter 7p per book. Overseas: 60p for the first book and 18p per copy for each additional book.